MURDER

in

Margaritaville

An Alex Trotter Mystery

Cheryl Peyton

ISBN – 1508831289
ISBN – 9781508831280

This is a work of fiction. Names, characters, places and incidents are either the product of the author's imagination, or are used fictitiously. Any resemblance to any actual persons, living or dead, is entirely coincidental.

This book was printed in the United States of America, 2015.

Cover photo by Cheryl Peyton

Other Books by Cheryl Peyton

Six Minutes to Midnight

Walk on Through the Rain: A Polio Survivor's Story

Murder on Bedford Island – An Alex Trotter Mystery

Murder on the Bermuda Queen – An Alex Trotter Mystery

Available at www.amazon.com in soft cover and eBooks
In soft cover at www.barnesandnoble.com
Available as signed copies through the author's website:
www.cheryljpeyton.com and
www.authorsguildoftn.org

Murder

in

Margaritaville

An Alex Trotter Mystery

Chapter One

ALEX PEERED UP through her windshield at the pillowy grey sky as she drove south on Lake Shore Drive. Snow was in the forecast, as was typical for January in Chicago, but it wasn't expected to be heavy lake-effect accumulation; just a couple of inches of the dry, flyaway variety. Nothing to be concerned about. Nothing, at least, for native Chicagoans like Alex who were proud of taking bad weather in stride. Bad weather and the Cubs.

The nickname, "Windy City," was coined in the late nineteenth century, referring to the rambling speakers at political conventions at the time. But the name stuck, thanks to the stiff breezes that regularly blew off the lake to batter pedestrians on Michigan Avenue, and on the bridges over the Chicago River.

On this day, Alex wasn't worried about harsh weather, or driving in a little snow, as she didn't have that far to go. The trip from her near north side apartment, to client Flossie Quill's home in Oak Park, should take less than an hour with light traffic on a Sunday afternoon.

She would be meeting with members of Flossie's Oak Park Authors League, or "OPAL," who had signed up to attend the annual Key West Literary Seminar.

As their tour director, Alex had made their travel arrangements and would accompany them down to the island, escort them on local excursions, and take care of their needs while they were there.

Shuddering with a sudden chill, she turned up the car heater, which reminded her that a few days in the sub-tropics would be a much-welcomed break from the harsh wintry weather.

As she drove, large snowflakes began swirling in front of her. Before long, enough of them had stuck to her windshield that she had to turn on the wipers.

By the time she got on the Eisenhower, or "Ike" as it was known locally, visibility had decreased substantially and snow was accumulating on the pavement. Fortunately, salt trucks were already out on the job, although what they were spreading mixed with the snow and sent up thick walls of spray onto the cars, coating them with a grey syrupy mixture.

After exiting onto Oak Park Avenue, she tried in vain to see out her side window to make out some house numbers. Since it was still early, residents hadn't yet turned on their porch lights, which further hampered her efforts.

Just as she lowered her window a few inches to get a clearer view, she heard a whooshing sound as her hair was sucked out the crack and slapped against the roof, while her face was pelted with snow.

"Geez, Louise!" Rattled now, she fumbled around blindly for the window controls, but punched all the door locks, instead, evidenced by the clicking sounds as the wind and snow continued blowing inside the car.

"Enough already!" Defiantly, she stabbed at her window button, which quickly restored a measure of calm. Driving on, she hastily brushed off her face with a wet glove, and made a couple of half-hearted swipes at the white blanket on the dashboard.

Driving was now becoming more hazardous, due to her limited vision as well as the reduced width of the pavement caused by old snowbanks.

In the middle of the next block, she slowed and barely cracked open her window to look for a number again. Seeing a stately Queen Anne house that had a plaque near the curb, she eased up and stopped to read it. The address was 339 Oak Park Avenue, identified as the "Birthplace of Ernest Hemingway." *Hmmm. Interesting coincidence,* she thought. Her client was a known author who lived on the same street and within two blocks of where the late prize-winning author had been born.

It occurred to her that Hemingway may have been the inspiration for the founding of OPAL, since all of the members lived in his home city. She was anxious to meet this group who, she knew, wrote in many different genres, from childrens literature, to crime stories and thrillers.

As she drove along, her mind went back to when she first met the elderly, refined Flossie Quill, who was ironically the author of steamy Gothic romances, full of graphic sex and violence. Flossie had shown her a few of them. From the synopses on the back covers, she saw that their plots always involved a beautiful heroine being held against her will and mistreated in some gloomy castle. At the end of the book, the despairing young woman would be finally rescued by a dashing young prince with whom she would fall instantly in love, have loin-rippling sex, and ride off with to live happily ever after.

Glancing at her watch, Alex saw that it was seven minutes to three. She should be on time, although she still had to find a place to park. and that could be her undoing. What with the snow piled up against the curbs, and the few shoveled-out areas being "reserved" with old kitchen chairs and brooms, there wasn't much space left. "Reserving" wasn't a legal maneuver, but it was a time-honored practice by urban dwellers who felt entitled to control the pavement immediately in front of their addresses.

In the middle of Flossie's block, Alex spotted a few feet of unoccupied curb space abutting a private drive where no one had dared park. Looking at the distance, she calculated that she could park her Fiat there without hanging over onto the inviolable driveway.

Wiping down her window with her coat sleeve, she peered out and was surprised to see that Flossie's house was the Victorian building right across the street. That cinched it. Pulling up behind the next parked car, she turned off the ignition and silently congratulated herself that she had made it safety, on time; and had snagged a legal parking space.

Flipping down her visor mirror, her self-satisfaction evaporated as she caught sight of her ravaged face. Black mascara had been streaked under her eyes and smeared onto her cheeks. In addition, her long, curly hair was now dampened, some stuck to the sides of her head, while the rest was standing up on end.

Digging through her purse, she unearthed tissues and lipstick to make a few hasty repairs before patting down her ginger-colored hair, which was unruly in the best of circumstances, and totally frizzed out when exposed to high humidity.

14

Glancing at the results, she was satisfied that, at least, she no longer resembled Alice Cooper, and snapped the visor back in place before she changed her mind.

Picking up her briefcase and purse off the passenger seat, she slid out of the car and stood leaning against her door to consider her next move.

After taking a moment to rearrange herself, she tied her long wool muffler around her neck, hung her purse over one shoulder, and slung her briefcase over the other.

Then, teetering on high heels, she started across the street taking baby steps to keep from slipping on the new layer of snow over unseen icy patches.

But, just as she reached the other side, a gust of wind blew her scarf over her face throwing her off balance. While she was windmilling her arms to try to stay on her feet, the heavy briefcase pulled her over to one side, causing her to tumble backwards into a snowbank.

"God Bless America!" she shrieked, flat on her back. Letting her frustration dissipate for a moment, she slowly regained rational thought, remembering her clients who were waiting inside for her, looking forward to hearing more about their trip. Resolutely, she pushed her hands into the snow, gained enough support to sit up, get her feet under her, and stand back up.

Once on her feet, she vigorously shook out her coat and stamped her feet. Then, picking up her purse and case, she set her chin and started again for the house. With the snow coming towards her, stinging her face, her only thought was that the trip to warm, sunny Key West couldn't come soon enough.

Sunday afternoon

Chapter 2

STANDING IN FRONT of Flossie Quill's door, she took a couple deep breaths to compose herself, patted down her hair, and brushed off her coat again. Maybe no one had been looking out the window while she was making a 'snow angel' in the front yard; but, before she could even press the bell, Flossie had thrown open the door, dispelling that notion.

Nevertheless, her hostess seemed unruffled and smiled broadly in welcome. Alex could only envy how warm and dry the woman looked in her thick cream-colored shawl and tweed skirt.

"Come in! Come in! You'll catch your death! Would you like a towel to dry yourself off, dear?"

"Oh, no, I'm fine," Alex muttered, looking down at her feet where she was dismayed to see a dirty puddle forming. "Uh, I'll take off my shoes. Where can I put them?"

"Oh, nonsense. These old floors have seen much worse than a little water." She paused, screwing up her mouth in thought. "Well, maybe not worse, but let me have your coat. This snow is so tiresome, isn't it? I've got a nice fire going inside, and there are refreshments in the dining room. I'll take you in and introduce you. The members who've signed up are all here and anxious to hear about your plans, I'm sure. There are ten of them and one spouse, as you know."

Removing her wet coat, Alex cringed when Flossie gingerly took hold of it by its collar and carried it off at arm's length over to the wardrobe.

Having a moment, Alex looked around the spacious entry hall. Suspended from the ceiling was a graceful abalone light fixture. On the long wall sat an impressive carved console with a heavy gold-framed mirror above it. Toile paper covered the walls, and small black and white tiles were laid on the floor in an old-fashioned pattern.

Flossie returned and tucked her hand under Alex's elbow, steering her towards the doorway. "Let's go in and get you settled with some nice hot tea, or wine, and something to eat. Then you can take your time to get acquainted with everyone before you give your little talk about the trip.

Giving Alex's arm a little squeeze, she enthused, "I can't wait until you meet our dear Matthew Evans. I think he'd be so perfect for you! He's a lovely young man, and a good writer, too. He sets some of his stories in exotic locales; places you probably know, that most people don't."

"Oh, I'm sure I'll like everyone, Flossie, but I've told you about my boyfriend–"

"I know, I know," Flossie demurred. "The homicide detective down south you said would be joining us for the last couple of days." She rounded her mouth into a little moue. "Well, anyway –" she waved away her thought.

As they stepped inside, Alex looked around at the people who had congregated in the formal parlor, either sitting or standing, while they chatted with plates of food in their hands.

Flossie cleared her throat. "May I have your attention, please? Your attention, please!" The room quieted. "Thank you. This lovely young lady is Alex Trotter of Globe-Trotter Travels whom I've told you about. You can all introduce yourselves to her after she has a chance to catch her breath. And, in a little while, she'll tell us about our trip to Key West and answer any questions, I'm sure. I've found that she's very thorough."

Alex had met with Flossie in person only once, but had been in touch by phone several times over the past few weeks to discuss the group's preferences and interests. Since then, Alex had made all the necessary reservations. She planned to go over some of the particulars today, have them sign the travel documents, and pay the balance on their accounts.

Flossie now led her into the wainscoted dining room where a damask-covered table held plates of delicacies that would have been suitable for an English high tea: fancy finger sandwiches, scones with jam and clotted cream, bowls of strawberries, miniature éclairs, and petit fours. A silver tea service sat at one end, while chilled bottles of Prosecco and stemware had been set up at the other end.

After Alex filled her plate with a sampling of each treat, and poured herself a cup of tea, she followed Flossie back to the parlor where her hostess indicated that they sit on the sofa next to the fireplace. From her spot, Alex found that she could angle her legs to get close enough to the fire to feel the drying warmth on her cold wet feet.

Taking a moment to look around the room, she saw that it not only reflected the owner's taste, but her occupation as well. Stuffed bookcases lined one wall, while the other three were hung with Romantic-themed paintings of turreted castles, Venetian canals, and moonlit gardens.

As Alex nibbled on her food and sipped her tea, she had a chance to more closely observe the people in the room. In particular, two women who were talking together drew her attention. One of them was stroking a beaver hand puppet, while the other one carried a basket on her arm that had a girl doll in it. Besides the oddity of bringing children's toys to an adult get-together, she was struck by the fact that the toys bore a close resemblance to their owners. The woman with the beaver puppet had a pronounced overbite and wore her brown hair pulled back into a low pony tail, while the doll lady had small features and staring blue eyes.

Intruding on her thoughts, Flossie leaned in and companionably patted her knee. "While we have a minute, dear, I'll point out who's who."

"That'd be nice, Flossie. Why don't you start with the woman with a beaver on her hand, and her friend with the doll?"

"Yes, well that would make sense. Okay. That's Grace Tuttle with Benny the Beaver, and that's Frances Primm with Trixie. They write childrens books." She snorted a little. "I guess you didn't think they wrote science fiction, for heaven's sake."

Alex chuckled. "Let's just say I'm glad to hear they write for children. But to state the obvious, there aren't any *children* here."

"True. I don't know why, but Grace always has Benny on her hand, as far as I know. I swear she thinks he's real. She opens his mouth to have him 'talk' and animates him to make him look like he's alive." Flossie made circles next to her head with her index finger.

"And Frances is the same way. She takes that doll everywhere she goes. She says she keeps it with her to be ready to read 'Trixie stories' to kids. To be fair, she does often go to schools. The doll's mischievous adventures are meant to teach children that bad behavior has consequences. I just hope the kids don't get more inspiration from Trixie's tricks.

"Anyway, don't be surprised if Frances and Grace bring their 'little friends' down to Key West." She threw up her hands while rolling her eyes.

"Let's see – who else? Oh, see the two women seated in that corner? That's Cynthia Hart in the lace-trimmed blouse, and Adeline Bloom in the floral dress. Adeline *always* wears floral prints. And she's even more flowery in her writing. We think of her as Add-A-Line. Kind of cute, isn't it?" she giggled.

Alex smiled in amusement. "That's pretty good. But, let me guess – Hart and Bloom are Romance writers."

Flossie threw back her head and whooped, "You're right! But they don't write Gothics like mine." She paused. "You know, it's kinda odd, but the three of us who write steamy love stories are all single."

Her eyes then lost their sparkle. "Actually, I *was* married. Forty-one years. My husband died a couple years ago. But we had many good years together." She puckered her lips in thought. "Well, anyway ..." she shook her head and pulled her shawl closer around her.

"Well, where was I? Oh, yes. The man in the leather vest is Jack Burns, and the younger man with him is Matthew Evans, who I was telling you about. Isn't he handsome? And he's such a sweetheart."

Alex was still focused on the older man whose lanky frame looked uncomfortably folded into one of

Flossie's dainty settees. "Jack Burns looks just like Ernest Hemingway! The beard, the ruffled hair. Everything. Too bad we won't be down in Key West for their annual 'Hemingway Look-Alike' contest. He'd be a shoo-in. Oh, and speaking of Hemingway, I noticed that his birthplace is just down the street."

"Oh, yes, we're all into Ernest Hemingway around here. Of course, we'll want to see his home in Key West. Since you mentioned it, Jack is more like Hemingway than just his looks. He's led a pretty wild life, too. He's a semi-retired newspaper man – you know, how Hemingway started out. Nowadays, Jack writes a few features, and his books, of course – high adventure, spy stories, crime novels; that kind of thing. He's quite a character. Married and divorced three times. But you're supposed to be interested in Matthew Evans."

Alex glanced over at the younger man. Unlike Jack, Matthew's face was unlined and clean-shaven. He was undeniably attractive with his high, smooth forehead, even features, and thick dark hair. But he lacked the lines of worldly experience that were etched into the older man's face. "He *is* very nice looking. Are he and Jack good friends?"

Flossie screwed up her mouth in thought. "Sure, they're friends. To look at it another way, Jack doesn't hold much truck with the rest of us; like the Romance writers and children's authors, in particular. Of the people here, I'd say maybe he's okay with Marla Page, who writes thrillers, and Ethan O'Leary, who writes science fiction. I don't think Jack's exactly chummy with Virgil Meade, either. He's our one poet – a very high-minded literary sort.

Her face suddenly brightened. "Oh, here's Virgil now – Virgil! Come over here for a moment. I'd like you to meet Alex."

Alex studied the pale, balding man as he shuffled over to greet her. Once there, he extended a limp hand that emerged from a worn corduroy sleeve. "It's my pleasure, Miss. What a wonderful profession you have. I know that you're a lot younger than me, but you've undoubtedly seen more of the world than I have." His brow furrowed as he looked up at the ceiling. "I don't know who it was who said, 'The world is a book and those who do not travel read only one page,' but that about sums it up, doesn't it?"

Alex smiled obligingly. "I haven't heard that before, but I know that reading can transport a person to many other places. I admire someone like *you* who can write poetry. You even have a poet's name, right?"

"Yes, although the poet we know as Virgil was actually Publius Vergilius, so I'm lucky that I wasn't named Publius." He chuckled at his little joke that Alex thought he had probably made many times before. "But I am proud to have the name of a man who influenced all of Western literature through one poem; not that anyone outside of a high school Latin class has ever read the *Aeneid.*"

Alex only hoped that he wouldn't quiz her on it. She thought that it had something to do with the founding of Rome; or was that by Romulus and Remus? Or were they characters *in* the *Aeneid?* Time to change the subject.

She cleared her throat. "Uh, well, I'm sure you'll be inspired by the beauty and spirit of Key West. It's the only place I know of where they celebrate every sunset with an arts festival. It's an old tradition that was brought back by the Cultural Preservation Society in the 1970s."

Virgil Mead nodded distractedly. "Yes, I've heard of it. But I'm probably more interested in the image of the sun sinking into the silver sea behind silhouetted boats that bob on the waves."

Alex blinked and stared at the man. Noticing her expression, he mumbled, "I guess that sounds a little too fanciful. Of course, poets can find inspiration most anywhere. As Dorothy Sayers once said, 'Heaven deliver us, what's a poet? Something that can't go to bed without a song about it.'"

Flossie emitted a throaty chuckle. "That's a good one, Virgil. And that's what I like about your poetry. You can rhapsodize about the most commonplace things without getting all 'moon and June' rhyming about it.

"Anyway, it's been nice chatting with you, Virgil, but I think we better let Alex meet some of our other writers too." Virgil bowed slightly and moved off.

Flossie cupped her hand over her mouth as she nudged Alex ."You did very well with our Virgil. I'm sure you found him to be pretty Edwardian."

Edwardian? Alex put on her best wise-guy smirk and shrugged. *Yeah. Right. Totally Edwardian. What was this woman talking about?*

Flossie appeared to be satisfied with her response and took a sip of her wine. Leaning back, she scanned the room again. "Well, who would you like to meet next? Ethan O'Leary and his wife, Joan – or, how about Matthew Evans?"

Alex cocked her head and smiled bemusedly at the older woman. "I'm starting to see why you're such a good writer of Romances, Flossie. I really doubt that Matthew Evans is any more interested in me than I am in him. But I'll meet him. Don't worry.

"You've done a great job in getting me orientated as to who's in your little group, Flossie, but I think I'll walk around and meet the others on my own, if that's okay with you. After I get a glass of wine, of course. When do you think you'd like to start your meeting – about four o'clock? That'll give me like twenty minutes."

"That's fine with me, dear. If you take a little more time, what's the difference? Just let me know when you're ready."

***

AS SHE POURED HERSELF a flute of Prosecco, Alex was careful to hold the dripping bottle above the ice bucket. Holding her glass steady, she slowly walked back to the front parlor and glanced around. Catching the eye of Marla Page, the tall, thin woman with pinched features Flossie had pointed out, she smiled and made her way over.

"Hi. Flossie told me that you write crime novels. They're mysteries, right? Or is there a difference between the two? I guess I'm not really a sophisticated reader, but I enjoy mysteries."

Marla just stared back blankly, so Alex went on to fill the awkward pause with what she knew sounded like babble. "I mean, I'm not a great reader – well, I'd like to be if I had the time, of course – but I have read some British mysteries."

Marla Page screwed up her nose as though a bad smell had suddenly enveloped her. "Let me guess. Agatha Christie?"

Alex tried not to show offense at the obviously belittling remark. "Well, yes … among others … also, Sherlock Holmes."

"Sherlock Holmes is a *character* in a series written by Sir Arthur Conan Doyle."

Alex felt her face redden. "I know that. Anyway, let's talk about *your* books. What kind of mysteries, or crime novels, do you write? What's your latest, for instance?"

Marla rolled up her eyes. "My latest was reviewed in the Chicago Tribune last month – in the Sunday supplement. Michael Collins gave it four stars. Anyway, it's one of my dark thrillers titled, *Yelling Bloody Murder,* about a coed who's sexually assaulted at a party in her sorority house. The outcome is probably not what you would expect. I'll tell you this much – it isn't the coed who's doing the yelling. The story is pretty intense – not Agatha Christie, for sure. I have some copies in my car, if you think you're up to it."

Alex attempted to match the other woman's smug expression and affected voice. "I think I can handle it. In fact, after I read it, I'll probably share it with my boyfriend who's a homicide detective. See how true-to-life he finds it. Actually, I've assisted him in investigating a couple of murders, so ..."

Alex had the satisfaction of seeing Marla's jaw drop open. "Anyway, have you been down to the Literary Seminar before, or to Key West at all?"

Marla Page was still off-balance. "Uh, no, I haven't done either. I was hoping my husband could go, but he's too busy with his practice. I thought I might as well go, anyway – with the group. After all, it's a major literary event. People come from all over the world to hear best-selling writers lecture and lead discussions on aspects of literature. This year the theme is, 'Real Emotions, Lasting Impressions.' Should be good. I know I love hearing from my readers that they find my stories so riveting and that my characters are memorable. And thanks to social media, my fan base keeps growing exponentially. In fact, I'm gratified to be able to say that I'm now considered an International author."

Alex was momentarily speechless. *Geez. Nothing wrong with this woman's ego.* Unable to resist being a little catty, she came back with, "I'm surprised that you haven't been invited to appear on the stage at the seminar."

Marla's small eyes bored through her. "There's only so much time and so many worthy authors. No one from OPAL has been selected. Neil LeRoy will be speaking, and he's a friend of our group. I'm sure you know his name − even though you're not a reader. He'll probably invite some of us more successful authors to share our knowledge with those who need help with marketing their projects."

Alex nodded. "Well, I'm sure you'll impress them as much as you've impressed me, Marla. If you'll excuse me, I need to move along, but I'll get your book before I leave. I don't think you'll forget, will you?"

***

Alex spent the next several minutes talking to the others, until she got around to Jack Burns and Matthew Evans. As she approached, the two men politely stood. She noticed that Jack was about three inches taller than Matthew.

"Thanks for coming," Jack greeted her. "Looking forward to hearing about Key West."

Alex raised one eyebrow. "I'd be surprised to learn that this would be your first visit, Mr. Burns."

"Oh, then you'd be surprised to hear how many places I haven't been. I've climbed Mount Kilimanjaro, but I haven't been to Mount Rushmore. And call me 'Jack,' by the way."

"Right. Jack. And speaking of Kilimanjaro, you must hear all the time how much you look like Ernest Hemingway. You'll attract a lot of attention on

26

the island where they venerate the man and keep his memory alive – along with the descendants of his cats, I might add."

He looked amused. "So I've heard. And, yeah, some folks have commented on the resemblance. I dunno. I write in Hemingway's simple, direct style. And I learned my craft the same way he did; writing for a newspaper. When you have to answer the five 'w's in the first paragraph of your piece, you learn how to get to the point. I leave the poetry to dudes like Vernon."

"Virgil," Matthew said out of the side of his mouth.

"Yeah. Virgil. Anyway, after making my bones on the City Desk, I was dispatched overseas as a foreign correspondent. That experience forever changed me. I found out how little I had known of the world. Now I'm being humbled again by trying to write novels, fictionalizing some of my experiences. Anyway, I assure you I'm no Hemingway, although I appreciate the comparison."

Alex drained her glass and set it on a nearby table. "Well, you must be a better writer than you are a salesman. Despite your modest opinion of your work, I think that I'd like to read one of your books– if you don't mind. Is there one in particular you'd recommend?"

Jack studied his loafers for a moment. Looking up, he wore a sheepish grin. "You make a good point that I should talk up my books if I expect anyone else to want to read them. What kind of books do you like?"

Alex shrugged. "Oh, I don't know . . . mysteries, adventure, suspense. What most people like."

He nodded. "Okay, how about one that's set in the Middle East, like my *Footprints in the Sand.* It's about some Bedouin nomads who live on the West Bank. There's a mystery at the heart of the story."

Matthew clamped a hand on Jack's shoulder. "You wouldn't go wrong with *any* of his books. He's a very good writer who I'm trying to model, but I'm way behind. I haven't had a career in journalism, for one thing."

Alex turned towards him, taking note of his pleasant expression and intelligent dark eyes. "Do you have other work besides writing?" she asked him.

"Yeah, I have a second non-profit job. I'm an artist, too. Graphic art as well as fine art – painting."

Alex grinned. "Ha! I hate to sound like a copycat, but I tried to make a living as an artist before going into the travel business. Did you go to the Art Institute, by chance?"

"Of course. You?"

"Of course. We'll have to compare notes later. So, are you going to the seminar to concentrate on writing, now?"

"Oh, I guess I'm going to hear Jack's friend Neil LeRoy, who's one of the featured speakers. I'm a big fan of his. And I'd like to show him some of my graphic art, as well as the other authors there, to try to get some cover design work."

Alex nodded. "Oh, yeah. That's a good idea. I heard about Neil LeRoy from Marla Page. She said he's a friend of the group. Is he an honorary member or something?"

Jack guffawed. "Neil, a member of OPAL? He doesn't need a group like ours to get recognition. And I'd be surprised if Marla's ever met the man. I got to know him in Beirut at the end of the Lebanon hostage crisis in '92. That's when he left the diplomatic service and started writing spy novels. *Best-selling* spy novels.

"By the way, Matthew here is a helluva writer, especially for *our* group. You need to read one of his books. Try G*one.* It's about a little boy who goes missing. From his own room. You won't be able to put it down."

Jack scanned the room with a furrowed brow. "We don't have many true literary writers here. We have writers of romance who use phrases like 'rippling muscles' and 'heaving bosoms.' And we have a couple women who write children's books with talking animals." He shook his head and leaned in towards her. "Now, I'm all for writers who use their imaginations; that's what we're all about. But I have to draw the line at talking to a fur-covered hand. Or to a doll."

Alex snickered. "Actually, I *did* have a conversation with Benny the Beaver. Grace Tuttle voiced his complaint to me that there aren't any beavers in Key West.

"I told him – or Grace – that I wasn't aware of that. What else can you say about that? It was a strange conversation. Why would Grace have done research on beavers in Key West? I mean, she doesn't have a *beaver*. She has a puppet. And why bring the puppet to an adult party?" Alex clamped her hand over her mouth. "Oh, I shouldn't be gossiping like this. I don't even know the woman. It's totally unprofessional and indiscreet. I'm sorry."

Jack shrugged. "Don't apologize to *me*. Hell, I'm always indiscreet. Besides, if you go around with a talking puppet like you're Shari Fucking Lewis, when you're not even a ventriloquist, you have to expect people talking about you."

Matthew laughed out loud. "Don't worry, Alex. We'll all get along okay in Key West. We have some unusual personalities, but they're all good people."

Jack looked dubious. "Yeah, well you haven't been on a trip with any of them. Like Mark Twain said, 'there's no better way to find out whether you like people or hate them is to travel with them.'"

Alex waved off his concern. "I'm used to taking people on trips who don't even know each other and they all get along. (She crossed her fingers thinking of the couple of murders that had occurred on past trips. They were the exceptions that proved the rule. Besides, no need to make an announcement and upset people.) She forced a smile. "I try to make sure that everyone has enough personal space and free time to reduce stress. Also, it helps if everyone's kept comfortable and pampered.

"Which reminds me, I seem to remember that the characters in Mark Twain's *Innocents Abroad* sailed around Europe on an old Civil War boat, didn't they? Not too comfortable."

Matthew elbowed his friend. "She's got you there, Jack."

Alex didn't betray her self-satisfaction as she coolly glanced at her watch. "I see it's after four so I should go and get Flossie to start our meeting. I've enjoyed talking to you guys. I'll have to get your books, too."

She hustled away thinking, *Thank you Miss Wallace for the American Lit assignment that just saved my butt. Geesh, how am I going to keep up with these people? I'm about out of literary references and I've only been with them for an hour.*

Looking around, she saw that Flossie was talking to Frances Primm who was holding Trixie in her arms. She headed over to join them, trying to avoid the doll's glassy stare.

Was it her imagination, or did the doll's eyes just blink? She felt the hairs stand up on the back of her neck. Looking away from the doll, she tried to sound calm. "Hi, ladies. Flossie, I just wanted to tell you that I'm ready for our meeting to start whenever you are."

"Oh, fine, dear. Frances – why don't you and Trixie take the last seat on that sofa over there so you both have a good view."

Alex bit down on her lower lip, assessing the woman's sanity.

Flossie trilled a laugh. "Ha! I'm just kiddin', Alex. We tease Frances about treating the doll like she's a person. Did you see her basket? Frances says it has to be low enough for Trixie to look out. Isn't that a hoot?"

Alex shuddered, but managed to pull back her lips into a passable smile.

Frances was staring at her. "You should see your face, Miss Trotter. You look like you've seen a ghost. Relax. Trixie's just a toy." She held up the doll up. "See? She's just china and fabric. She comes alive in my books, so I treat her like she's real for the kids' sakes. I think they'd be very upset if they saw me taking her out of a suitcase. Here, hold her. She's really quite cuddly." She lifted up the doll close to Alex's face.

Alex took her, but quickly turned her around so that she faced Frances. "Of course, she's a nice doll. I guess Flossie's comment just reminded me of those scary dolls in the movies – you know, like Chuckie. I always had baby dolls as a kid. Their eyes were painted on. Trixie's eyes open and close, right?"

"Only when you lay her on her back. And she's certainly nothing like the demon-possessed dolls in the movies," she snapped.

"Oh, no. Of course she's not. And I didn't mean to make any such comparison. I'm sorry that I didn't get that Flossie was teasing."

Frances didn't smile. "Fine. Let's leave it at that, then. I guess you two need to get the meeting started. Here, I'll take back Trixie."

After Frances took her back, Alex was embarrassed to admit to herself that she felt relieved.

Chapter 3

FLAMES DANCED ON THE LOGS behind Flossie as she started the meeting. After running through some items of "housekeeping," she briefly described Alex's background and what she would be handling for them on their upcoming trip. Finally, she asked Alex to come up and speak.

Taking Flossie's place, Alex began, "Well, thanks for signing up and taking me out of Chicago for a few days in January. I promise you that Key West will average 85 degrees when we're there." This was met with applause and some expressions of relief.

"Flossie told me that you wanted to stay in a hotel with character that's in Old Town, to be close to the restaurants, stores and night life. I'm happy to be able to tell you that we will be staying at the C'est la Vie on Duval Street – at a special rate. Besides it being in the middle of downtown, it's within walking distance of the San Carlos Institute where your Literary Seminar will be held." There were pleased murmurings from the group.

"The building dates from 1892. It's in the classic Key West style, built of white clapboard with a pillared front porch, shuttered windows, and roof gables that create those little sitting nooks in the top-story. Rooms in the two wings off the back overlook the courtyard that is planted in lush tropical landscaping.

"It's one of about 3,000 frame structures built in the 19th century that still stand today on the island. Most of them look like Early American colonials, because they were built by New Englanders who were the first settlers. Fortunately, they used pine wood from Dade County, which is hard enough to withstand even hurricanes.

"In the 1920s, the city realized that these old buildings could be valuable as tourist attractions, so they set up an architectural committee to protect them. And, in the 1990s, these homes were credited for the beginning of a tourist boom in Key West that continues on today.

"I've brought brochures of the hotel that'll show you its façade, a couple of rooms, and the courtyard. Also, it lists and describes its amenities. Flossie, why don't you take one and pass the rest around."

Flossie took the stack and held one up to examine it. "Oh, this is lovely, dear. Could be the setting for one of Cynthia's or Adeline's romances. Or even one of Marla's murder mysteries."

Marla snickered derisively. "Yeah, if the place is haunted."

Alex shook her head. "I don't think so, but there's no lack of houses in town that claim to be. There are tours through them, if you're interested."

Glancing around the room she added, "I think you'll find a lot of inspiration in Key West for your writing. There's a history of piracy and sunken treasures, political rebellion, a colorful Latin influence, and the free-spirited residents. Of course, the most familiar image of the City's laid-back life style is Jimmy Buffet's 'Wasted Again in Margaritaville.'

"And that brings me to the nightlife – that actually starts at eleven in the morning when the bars open for business, and stay open until four in the morning. One of the most popular clubs is the 'Some Like it Hot' lounge that's connected to our hotel and features female impersonators as a draw.

"Don't worry, the noise shouldn't be a problem in your rooms. The hotel's designed so that the public rooms are in front, while most of the guest rooms are behind, facing the courtyard. Of course, if you do hear music that bothers you, let me know. The hotel staff will make some adjustments for you.

"The C'est la Vie is a pretty casual place, but their services and accommodations are first-class. I assure you they don't answer you with, 'That's Life,' as their name would suggest, if you do have a complaint."

She glanced down at her notes. "Moving on, I just want to give you a little history of the island so you can better appreciate what you'll see there. Let's start with the name 'Key West.' It comes from the original Spanish name– Caya Hueso. As you probably know, 'k-e-y' is the anglicized version of 'c-a-y,' meaning 'small island.' And you probably think that 'West' refers to the fact it's the most western island along the Gulf coast, which it is – it's also the most southern point in the United States, but that's another story.

"The Spanish settlers named the island 1,000 years ago, before there were any maps that would have shown the island's location. The origin of the name actually came from the bones of the enemies of the Calusa Indians that they found on the beach. The

35

Spanish for bones, is 'huesos' with the 'h' sounding like our 'w.' When English-speaking people moved to the island in the early 19th century, they went by the sound of the Spanish name and wrote it down as 'Key West.'"

"Isn't that interesting, dear?" Flossie inserted. "Although I don't think the island would have quite the same appeal today if it were called 'Bones Beach,' although that sounds like 'Jones Beach' which is so popular on the East Coast. But, what is the significance of Key West being the most southern point in the country?"

Alex nodded. "In its history, their southern location has been an influence on the City's character.

"By 1831, the U.S. government had built a naval station and army post in Key West to protect it as a U.S. Territory. When the Civil War broke out, the Federal government stayed in control of the forts and the City, with the result that Key West was the *only southern city* to stay in the Union after the south seceded, even though some of the residents were southern-sympathizers. Stranger still, the naval base set up a blockade *against* confederate ships and captured about 200 of them and brought their owners and sailors to trial after the end of the war.

"Then, in the 1870s, thousands of Cubans started immigrating to the island to escape the revolution against Spanish colonial rule in their own country. Many became successful by establishing a profitable cigar industry on the island. By 1873, Cuban people were in the majority in the population.

Alex checked her notebook again. "Here's an interesting statistic. By 1890, Key West was the largest city in Florida having over 18,000 people at a time when Miami had under a thousand. In fact, Key West remained the largest city in the state until the 1920s.

Today, the population is about 25,000, following a decline in the mid-century, and an increase in the 1990s.

"One other interesting date for Key West is 1898 when the *USS Maine* sailed from there to Havana to protect American interests. Soon after, the battleship in the harbor was destroyed in an explosion in its gunpowder magazines that killed two-thirds of its crew. What was unknown then, and remains unknown, is how it happened, and who was responsible. Americans were outraged over the incident and blamed the Spanish, so a few months after the explosion the United States entered into the Spanish-American War. As a result of winning the war, the United States became a world naval power and acquired the territories of the Philippines, Guam, and Puerto Rico; and Cuba became independent."

Alex checked her watch. "Well, maybe that's enough history. I don't want to bore you with too many dates."

Looking around to gauge the interest of her audience, she was pleased that everyone seemed engaged, except for Grace Tuttle who was opening Benny's mouth into a yawn. Glancing at Frances and Trixie, it appeared that the doll's eyes were staring up at her, accusingly.

Alex felt herself getting hot. *I've got to get away from here. These 'toys' are giving me the creeps. Or their owners are – or both.*

She said, "Actually, that's probably enough information about Key West, for now. I've planned for us to take the tram tour on Monday afternoon after we're settled. The guides are very entertaining and informative, and the route will give you an overall view of the area and what you might want to go back to.

In addition, I've made up a list of places and activities I'm recommending that can be worked into your schedule, if you're interested. They're in your packets that I'll be handing out in a minute. I have a copy of your seminar program, but you probably don't know now what sessions you'll want to attend until the event gets underway. Also, I'm passing out your plane tickets for the round-trip flight out of O'Hare in about two weeks."

I do need to finalize the rooms before I leave today. Flossie mentioned that some of you would like to share, is that right? That won't be a problem as several of the rooms have two double beds."

Cynthia Bloom called out, 'Adeline and I would like to share a room. Hopefully, one facing the courtyard."

"Okay, fine. Anyone else?"

Grace Tuttle held up Benny to get her attention. Alex gripped her notebook and held her breath. "Yes, Grace?"

Giving a nod to Benny she said, "We'd like to share with Frances and Trixie."

Alex thought to herself, *Egads, the four of them in the same room for a week! Maybe Trixie will kill off the beaver or vice versa.* "Uh, fine, Grace. I'll take care of that."

She cleared her throat and looked around. "Anyone else? None of the men, then, right?"

Ethan O'Leary raised an index finger like he was bidding at an auction. "Uh, you probably have my wife and me down for one room."

Joan O'Leary laughed lightly, "I don't think Miss Trotter is asking who you'll be sharing with, Ethan."

Alex smiled at the pleasant-looking woman, gratified that she would be joining the tour.

"It would have been my first guess, Ethan, but thanks for clarifying," Alex responded.

"I'll pass out the packets I've put together with land and sea tours I'm recommending that you can read over before we leave. Any questions, now? No? Okay, well, I guess I'll see you next at O'Hare in about two weeks."

Flossie stood up and put an arm around her as the group applauded. "Thank you, dear. This was most interesting. Should be an exciting time for all of us."

Sunday evening

Chapter 4

"YOU HAVE TO ADMIT, you get the craziest people on your trips," Beth declared from her perch on the blue chenille chair.

Alex had spent the last hour relating her impressions of the OPAL authors to her roommate, ending with her descriptions of Frances Primm and Grace Tuttle and their mascots.

Alex sat with her feet curled under her on the sofa as she regarded her friend. "I'm sure I don't get the *craziest* people, Beth. And let's try to be fair to Frances and Grace. They write successful childrens books. You have to be rational to do that."

Beth cocked her head in inquiry "What about the fact that they take stuffed toys with them wherever they go and make believe they're real? That's not crazy?"

"Well, hold on a second, Dr. Phil, before you make a diagnosis. As Frances explained it, she treats the doll like it's real for the *children's* sakes. I mean, that makes *some* sense," she argued, not sounding convinced, herself.

"Yeah, sounds reasonable, except for the fact that there wasn't a child *within a mile,*" Beth emphatically countered, her ponytail swinging.

"That's true. Actually, I said the same thing to Flossie. As I told you, she's a nice grandmotherly sort, and she thinks the two women have just become caught up in their own imaginary worlds; although Grace also works as a nurse in the real world.

"Thinking about them when I was driving home, it occurred to me that they just might be putting us all on. I mean, it's fun for Grace and Frances to hide behind their props. It's like when adults dress up for a Halloween party. Being in costume gives people cover to act any way they want. Remember Halloween last year when you went to the party as Miley Cyrus?"

Beth groaned, bending over, holding her face between her hands. "Oh, please! Don't remind me. I'm still embarrassed about that. I can't believe that I was twerking in front of people that I see every day at work."

Taking a deep breath, she looked up at Alex. "In my defense, the theme was 'Halloween Party in the U.S.A.,' so I wasn't the only 'Miley' there. But you could have told me that I'm not 22 anymore, and that my ass isn't all that cute."

"I figured you knew that."

"Oh, thanks."

Alex chuckled. "Seriously, you should just forget about whatever you did that night. Everyone else was probably just as uninhibited. And I'm assuming there was some alcohol involved, right?" Beth gave a little snort. "Okay. So the other people probably don't even *remember* what you did, and just regret whatever they did."

"That's a comforting thought, Alex. And at least it was just the one night. That's way different from your ladies who are in disguise every day. That's what's crazy."

Alex unfolded her legs and stretched them. "You have a point there. Although I would have to say that Frances and Grace seem perfectly normal, except for walking around with a doll and beaver all the time."

"Hah! That's like saying Lizzie Borden was a loving daughter, except for that one time when she took an axe to her parents."

Alex looked up at the ceiling. "Well I'm glad you're not given to exaggeration, anyway. Speaking of which, that reminds me of something I haven't dared to tell you about Trixie. Probably because I didn't want you to think I'm crazy, too."

"What? Believe me, Alex, you're the sanest person I know. Besides, since you've gone this far, you have to tell me."

"Okay, okay. Just promise me you won't laugh." Beth only shrugged. "Well, here goes, anyway. First, I haven't really described Trixie so you can get the picture. She's one of those grown-up dolls."

"Like Barbie?"

"No, not like Barbie. She's bigger than that. I don't know what kind of doll she is. She's like an old-fashioned doll with a painted china face and creepy glass eyes like dolls you've seen in the movies that are possessed by an evil spirit. You know the kind I mean."

"Yeahhh. So – you think Trixie is possessed?"

42

"See? That's why I didn't tell you before. You think I'm crazy, too. No, I don't think the doll is *possessed*, but she did creep me out. At one point, I was walking over to talk to Frances when I swear I saw the doll blink at me. A little later, I was speaking in front of the whole group, and the doll's eyes moved up to stare at me."

Beth clamped her hand over her mouth to stifle her laughter. "Sorry, Alex, but that *is* crazy. Of *course* the doll's eyes moved. Those eyes are made to open and close. That's what you found disturbing? Not the woman who has a beaver puppet talk for her?"

Alex shook her head in exasperation. "You don't get it. First of all, the beaver has a cute face with button eyes and big buck teeth, and is obviously just a furry toy. Secondly, I asked Frances if the doll's eyes moved and she said they only close when she's laid on her back. Trixie was *sitting up* both times her eyes moved. That's why it was so weird. You would have thought so too."

Beth stuck out her lower lip in thought. "Okay, I can see how one of those dolls could be unnerving, but I think that Frances was playing with you. She must have dipped the doll backwards when you weren't looking, and later tilted up her head so it seemed like the doll's eyes were moving."

"You're probably right," Alex glumly agreed. "In fact, that's how I explained it to myself, but I kept doubting it because I was so unnerved at the time. Anyway, thanks for listening, Beth. I'm glad I told you. I feel more in control of my imagination just admitting to it."

She stood up. "I need to call Arlie and make sure he can still join me for the weekend in Key West."

Beth put down her coffee cup. "I wouldn't say too much about your group; he might change his mind."

Alex shrugged. "We'll see. I have to tell him *something*. No need to go into details, of course — although we've been through a lot worse things than putting up with a few eccentric authors."

"Yeah, like any of your other tours he's been on."

"Don't forget, I flew down to Atlanta to spend Christmas with his parents. I guess I can't ask him to fly to Paris to meet my parents at this point, but it's his turn to travel to see me. And don't worry about Arlie, Beth. This time we'll be in laid-back, tropical Margaritaville. He can totally relax and just 'nibble on sponge cake, watch the sun bake the tourists,' to paraphrase   the   song."

Later, Sunday evening

Chapter 5

ALEX LISTENED IMPATIENTLY to the phone's continual ringing on the other end. *Brnngg! Brnngg! Brnngg! C'mon, Arlie. Pick up.*

"Homicide. Arlie Tate here," the baritone voice drawled.

"You're at home, and that's how you answer the phone?"

"I knew it was you."

"Oh, you're so funny. Well, I'm calling like I said I would after meeting with the group going to Key West. Everything's all set. I hope you're still planning to come down for the last couple of days. And, remember, I flew down to Atlanta at Christmastime to be with you and meet your parents."

"You had a good time, didn't you?"

"Of course I did. Your parents couldn't have been nicer. But, still, I had to fly out of O'Hare at the busiest travel time of the year and I didn't complain.

And, remind me again, of all the nice things your mother said about me to you?"

"Alex, I'm a detective. I know when I'm being played. But, okay. She said that you're 'very pretty,' which you are; that you're 'utterly charming,' which you are only *some*times; and that 'I'm a lucky man,' which is debatable, considering the trouble your tour groups have caused me."

Alex squirmed in her chair. "I hope you didn't contradict your mother to her face. And I certainly hope you didn't tell her how we met on Bedford Island – that I was one of your murder suspects. Did you?"

"Yeah, as a matter of fact I did, but I put the best spin on it."

"There's no such thing as putting the 'best spin' on being accused of murder," she huffed. "Anyway, this conversation isn't going the way I'd hoped, so let's change the subject. Back to my original question; are you still able to join me in Key West … and do you still want to?"

"Of *course* I want to. Babe, I'm just havin' fun with you cuz you're so easy to tease. For the record, I'm looking forward to it. In fact, I've already arranged for the time, and I've got my plane ticket. And, hopefully, no one around here will become homicidal that week to change my plans. Speaking of murder, does this new group seem any less lethal than your last one?"

"Oh, for Pete's sake, Arlie, these people are serious writers."

"Clever dodge, dear, but non-responsive. I'm sure 'serious writers' can be jealous, or vengeful, or have any other motive people have when they murder somebody.

"So, tell me about your meeting. What're these people like?"

"Well ... they're all different, of course. And I've only just met them, so I can't tell you much. But, let's see ... they all seem very intelligent, and they're extremely well-read,, of course. In fact, they use literary quotes in casual conversation.

"I met with them at this house that's right down the street from Ernest Hemingway's birthplace. He's like their idol. One of the guys, Jack Burns, writes in the same concise style and even looks like him. I bought one of Jack's books about Bedouins, and a couple of the others' books.

"Which reminds me, I'm going to have to catch up on my reading in the next couple of weeks, and I'm about five years behind. You might want to read Jack's book after I read it. Come to think of it, I don't know what you read. Detective novels, I'm guessing."

Arlie chucked. "Not hardly. Try forensic journals."

"Oh."

"And history."

"Oh."

"You sound disappointed. Do you want me to wade through *The Sun Also Rises* before that weekend? I'm sorry, but I need to keep up with advances in criminology, and I like to read political history."

Alex brightened. "Oh, *politics*. That's something Jack writes about. He's been all over the world as a foreign correspondent. Like, he covered the hostage taker's crisis in Beirut in'92."

"Oh, well, we have something in common, then. I *shot* a couple of hostage takers in Atlanta in 2002. Do you think that'll help me fit in?"

"I'm not *comparing* you, Arlie. I was just fishing for reasons that you might enjoy spending a little time with these people."

"Don't worry about that, Alex. I'm going down there to spend time with you, not them. After I land on Friday afternoon, I hope we can go out for drinks and dinner. If you've got something planned with the group on Saturday and Sunday, I'll just tag along until you need to leave for the airport.

"At any rate, I'm not concerned about how I get along with your writers. I was just asking what you thought of them. In particular if there were any you thought might cause trouble; and I ask that because of past history.

"But, if they're all studious people who just read all the time, and you didn't notice anything to worry about, then I take your word for it."

Alex sat up straighter. "Okay. Let's go with that."

"Aha! I knew it. You're not telling me everything. In your groups, there's always some bully, or people who are feuding, or there are cheating spouses – something that could blow up on your tour."

Alex exhaled a long stream of air. "Oh, all right, I'll tell you, but it's nothing, really. It's just that the two women who write children's books unnerve me: Frances Primm carries around a demonic-looking doll that has eyes that move on their own, and Grace Tuttle has a beaver hand puppet that she animates and pretends is talking." Alex gritted her teeth and waited.

"Oh." Arlie seemed at a loss for words.

"Now *you* sound disappointed," Alex prompted. "I told you, it's nothing," she added to deflect her discomfort.

Arlie cleared his throat. "Well, I was thinking it would be more like someone threatening retaliation for plagiarism, or for putting bad reviews on Amazon. From what you're telling me, it doesn't sound all that odd if these toys are tied in with their books. And the women *were* at a meeting with fellow writers who know their books.

"If you want my opinion, which you may not, they sound pretty harmless to me. Maybe they identify too much with their characters, but that doesn't hurt anybody."

No response.

"Was there something else that bothered you?" Arlie asked more gently.

"Not really." Her voice was small. "Well, one mystery writer is obnoxious, the way she brags about herself and her books. Someone might want to kill *her*."

Arlie emitted a low chuckle. "Maybe we're looking too hard for potential trouble. In reality, they'll all be busy at the conference, and won't have a chance to get on each other's nerves. You'll probably have a lot of time on your hands to get a good rest and a tan. I wish I could join you for more than the weekend."

"I wish you could too, Arlie. Anyway, I can't blame Grace and Frances for freaking me out. Like the Buffet song says, 'It's my own damn fault.'"

"Hah. That's my girl. Use your sense of humor. And don't get cross-eyed, reading. You can hold your own in conversation with anyone. Seriously, I'm sure this trip will work out fine … but maybe call me when you get down there. Y'know, just to let me know that all's   well."

Monday noon, January 19

Chapter 6

THE SUN WAS HIGH overhead as Alex stood on the shaded two-story portico of the C'est La Vie hotel watching the OPAL members get off the airport transport bus. After stepping down, they stayed close to the curb to allow room for the oblivious tourists who took up most the sidewalk, walking three or four abreast.

By contrast, the authors looked distinctly self-conscious, wearing the dazed expressions and inappropriate clothing of people who had just arrived from a different climate and culture. Although the men had rolled up the cuffs of their long shirtsleeves, and the women had taken off their cardigan sweaters, everyone still had a tell-tale heavy coat draped over their arms.

While they stood there, uncomfortable in their clothes and unsure of what to do, the bus driver came around and wrenched open the door of the luggage compartment to get out their bags. Reaching in, he methodically started slinging suitcases out onto the pavement to be claimed by his passengers.

The first person to react to the pile-up was Matthew Evans, who stepped forward and impressively took hold and hoisted his bag over the other luggage in one fluid motion. Turning towards Flossie Quill, he asked, "Which one is yours, Mrs. Quill? I'll take it into the hotel for you."

"Oh, thank you, Matthew. You're always so kind and helpful. Uh, mine has a tapestry cover. There it is, next to that bright blue one."

She turned towards the hotel. "Oh, Miss Trotter waiting for us on the portico. Isn't this a lovely place she's found? She's such a charming and attractive woman, don't you think?"

Matthew was having enough trouble collecting several pieces of luggage to appraise the hotel and respond to Flossie's remarks with much more than a nod and a smile.

By now, the others had formed a circle around the luggage and were reaching over one another to pull out their bags, creating confusion and delays.

Seeing this, Alex slipped inside the hotel and soon emerged with two men in short-sleeved khaki uniforms. She called out from the top step, "Wait a minute! These gentlemen from the hotel will help you with your luggage so you can just go inside to check in."

Walking down to where they had congregated, she added, "If there are any problems, let me know. Otherwise, after you've settled in, I'd like you all to come back down to the lobby for our tram tour which will start at three o'clock outside the hotel. I promise you that this will be an enjoyable introduction to the island that you don't want to miss."

She went back up the steps to open the door for the others. Virgil Meade, looking paler than usual in a beige shirt and rumpled canvas hat, wrestled his suitcase up the stairs, stopped and turned to gaze out at the street.

Becoming aware of Alex standing nearby, he favored her with a wan smile. "Miss Trotter, this is a lovely old building, and a stimulating location. I was just now composing a haiku poem about it in my head. If you'll indulge me, I'll recite it for you."

Alex replied, "Sure, I'd like to hear it, as she leaned back against a pillar to get comfortable for his recitation.

Virgil cleared his throat, pulled back his shoulders and clasped his hands in front.

"Hot sun above
Deep shadows under cover
Facing east on Key West."

After he finished, she stood up straight, blinking in confusion. "Uh, is that it? Kinda short, isn't it?"

Virgil stared blankly at her. "Haiku is *always* a three-lined poem. The first line has five moras, or syllables, approximately; the next line has seven moras; and then five moras, again. Haiku is a poem that makes an observation about the contrasting essence of nature."

Alex smiled weakly. "I'm sorry, Virgil, but I guess I don't know much about haiku. I liked your images, but I'm more familiar with poems like limericks. One just popped into my head. Have you heard this one?

'There was an Old Man with a beard,
Who said, 'It is just what I feared!
Two Owls and a Hen,

Four Larks and a Wren,
Have all built their nests in my beard!'"

Virgil's mouth fell open as he gaped wide-eyed at her. "No, I don't believe I *have* heard that before." He looked up at the ceiling as though seeking divine assistance before he brought his attention back to her. "Uh, that *is* a fun little ditty, isn't it?" he managed in a strangled voice.

Alex patted down her hair that was frizzing up in the humidity. "Yes, I guess that's what it is. Not a serious work of art. Well, anyway, I won't keep you. Why don't you go in and register and get settled in your room. I hope to see you later for the tram tour."

Virgil made his escape just as Marla Page came tripping up the stairs wearing oversized sunglasses. Behind her one of the porters was struggling with a bulging suitcase and a designer garment bag. Frowning up at the inn she looked over at Alex. "Well, the place is old enough, that's for sure."

Alex answered dryly, "That's its charm. There's a Comfort Inn out by the airport for those who prefer uniformity and three-minute waffles."

Marla stuck her nose in the air. "Hmmph! There are other places to stay besides cheap motels and firetraps, although it's probably just as well we're staying in this relic; there can't be many fans here, so I can have some privacy, and be left alone."

"Oh, I think you can count on it." Marla tilted her head to one side considering the comment for a moment. Twisting her mouth, she yanked open one of the double doors and flounced inside, leaving the porter to get his foot off the threshold before the door closed on it.

Alex glanced at the bus. Grace and Frances were following the other porter who was pulling their suitcases and carry-on bags. Grace held her coat in one hand while wearing Benny on the other. Similarly, Frances carried Trixie in her basket, while her coat hung over her other arm.

After the threesome had mounted the steps, Alex opened the door for them, commenting, "I didn't realize you ladies had brought Benny and Trixie with you. I didn't see them on the plane."

Both women turned a baleful eye on her before Frances huffed, "They're the only reasons we're even here."

Grace held up Benny and said in a babyish tone, "My readers want to see me. And there'll be big people from major publishing houses, and television and movie people looking for a new star."

"O-kay, then." Alex took a step back. "I'll see you all later for the tram ride."

As she closed the door behind the two women, Ethan and Joan O'Leary walked up with their luggage. As Alex reached for the handle again, Joan leaned over and whispered, "Looks like you've got your hands full this week," nodding towards the departed France and Grace who had just entered the hotel.

Alex gave a little shrug. "Key West is like catnip to creative people with vivid imaginations. I wouldn't even *try* to predict what will happen this week.   Stay   tuned."

Chapter 7

AFTER ALL THE OPAL MEMBERS had checked in, and were presumably getting settled in their rooms, Alex embarked on a quick tour of the hotel.

The décor in the lobby set the style and the color scheme for the inn, with its deep gold walls set off by painted white woodwork, mahogany wood tables, overstuffed sofas in colorful chintzes, and pegged pine floors softened with rose Oriental rugs. The centerpiece of the room was a classic red brick fireplace, characteristic of the building's Colonial architecture, if not its tropical location.

Three hallways led away from the lobby, with a stairwell in the one behind. It rose up three floors, solidly built in dark wood with paneled wainscoting applied three feet high to protect the walls from being scuffed by suitcases being toted up and down the steps.

A small elevator was crammed into a corner across from the stairs. It appeared to have been a later addition to the space, probably to comply with revised public building codes to accommodate guests who weren't physically able to climb flights of stairs.

Alex opted to first take the hallway on the right, to follow the sign that pointed the way to the dining room. Walking a short distance, she came upon it. She opened the French doors and found herself in a large room that appeared to be decorated and set up for an English high tea. The ceiling was ornamented with fake wood beams, while the walls were papered in a small rose print. Dark wood tables, surrounded by spindle-backed chairs, were set with doily placemats. The tied-on gold chair cushions coordinated with the floral curtains at the mullioned windows. Hanging baskets with ferns added a natural element.

Alex assessed it for her group, thinking, *Well, the Romance writers will like this, but I'm not sure I can see Jack Burns being at home here.* At any rate, they all would be eating dinner together there only that night and the last night. At least the proper English setting should encourage good manners and polite conversation, which would be helpful considering the potential for discord among her people, she thought, glumly.

Leaving the dining room, she ventured further down the corridor until she came to a narrow staircase that twisted its way upstairs. Climbing up, she had to turn her feet sideways on the shallow steps and to hang onto the railing to give herself a little boost to surmount the steep grade.

When she got to the top, she entered into a rose carpeted hallway that was dimly lit by wall sconces. Each guest room doorway was recessed and identified with old-fashioned brass numbers.

The long, angled hallway ended in a "T" at another shorter hallway. Alex turned to the right to walk towards a lit exit sign where there was another stairway.   Descending one flight of steep stairs, she opened the door to a wide passageway.

The place was like a rabbit warren with all its hallways and stairs. *Where am I now?* she wondered, unsure of which direction to go. Spotting a window, she hurried over to look out, relieved to see the inner courtyard and its gardens outside.

Continuing down the hall, she came to an exterior door and went out into the sunshine. Looking across the way, she recognized the curly heads of Cynthia Hart and Adeline Bloom, changed into summery clothes, sitting on the edge of the fountain.

Approaching them she remarked, "I'm impressed that you were able to find this place. I've been wandering blindly down crooked hallways and up and down dark staircases all over the place."

Sitting down with them, she asked, "So, how do you like the C'est La Vie so far? How's your room?"

Cynthia Hart leaned back, stretching out her thin white arms along the concrete edge of the fountain. The elfin lines of her small face were turned up with pleasure. "I think it's all wonderful! Sitting here in the warmth of the sun makes me feel like I've emerged from a cocoon." She flapped her arms, presumably pantomiming a butterfly to demonstrate her imagery.

"It's actually *hot* here." Adeline said, fluffing her pink floral skirt like a fan over her pudgy calves. Her round face was flushed and glistened with perspiration. "But I love it. I love our room, too. It's decorated in Laura Ashley. Just my style.

"Since we're on the first floor and face the courtyard, it was easy enough to figure out how to get here. We didn't even bother unpacking, except to find something cool to put on."

Alex smiled and nodded. "I know what you're saying. I can't wait to get up to my room to get out of this heavy corduroy. I look like I'm dressed for a hayride." She shifted her gaze to the other wing of the hotel. "But I'm just noticing that screened porch over there that I want to check out first. I'll see you both later for the tram tour, okay?" The women nodded as she walked away.

On her way across the courtyard, she passed by stony-trunked palm trees, pink hibiscus bushes, and neat, mulched flower beds until she came to a screen door.

Inside, the air in the spacious high room was being cooled by three whirring ceiling. The porch was furnished with natural wicker sofas and chairs in tropical print cushions. A young couple sat close together on one of the sofas, hunched over guide books. They barely glanced up when Alex came in and walked around.

Leaving the porch, she found her way back to the small elevator behind the lobby. Getting in, she leaned back against the hand rail as the car started its slow ascent up to the third floor. Looking up, she noticed a sign reading, "MAXIMUM 6 PERSON OCCUPANCY," as well as a small camera mounted in a front corner.

After she got off, she walked halfway down the hall to arrive at her room. Unlocking the door and pushing it open, she took in the modest-sized, but airy room, with pale pink walls that slanted up to a high ceiling. The queen-sized bed was made up in a rose and green-print coverlet, with crisp white sheets and pillows. A window seat, built in under the dormer, was fitted with a plump dark green cushion that invited one to sit and look out at the passing parade of tourists on Duval Street.

The en suite bathroom was small, but clean, and adequately equipped. After splashing her face with cool water and patting it dry, she returned to the bedroom to kick off her shoes and lay back on the bed to unwind and review her situation.

So, here I am in Key West. Let me think...how do things stand? Nice weather... check; romantic tropical setting ... check; good restaurants ... check; plenty to do ... check; fun group ... uh, not exactly. There are a few oddballs – Frances and Grace, of course, and Virgil Meade is a little weird; and there's one real pill – Marla Page. Well, I've had worse, I guess. Anyway, it's almost time for the tram tour. That should put everyone in a good mood for the evening. One day at a time, girl. One day at a time.

Sunday afternoon.

Chapter 8

AT A QUARTER TO THREE, Alex came down to the lobby looking cool and refreshed in a short-sleeved yellow blouse, tan slacks, and sandals. Only her voluminous hair betrayed her exposure to high heat and humidity.

Glancing around, she was pleased to see some of the tour members were already there. Flossie, Cynthia and Adeline waved to her from the opposite corner. Virgil Meade hadn't noticed she was there as he was scrutinizing the millwork around the windows.

Starting to take a count, Alex saw that Jack Burns and Matthew Evans, standing by the fireplace, were talking to some man who wasn't with the group. He was tall and rangy with untidy brown hair and strong features who looked familiar, but she couldn't place him.

As she started over to introduce herself, Marla Page came from out of nowhere, knocking her aside, as she was making a beeline for the newcomer.

"Neil LeRoy! You're here!" she exclaimed, her arms outstretched to grab hold of her target.

At the sound of his name, the visitor glanced up, his eyes opening wide at the sight of Marla bearing down on him.

"I love your work," Marla effused, grasping his hand that he had held up defensively. "Your Nick Barnes character is so magnificently conflicted, almost schizophrenic, as he searches for his life's narrative between his role as an American federal agent, and his role as a spy."

"Nick Barnes does all that?" Neil LeRoy asked in dry tones.

Marla jutted out one bony hip, and struck a coy pose. "You're teasing me, I know. I'm just so pleased that you're in our group. I don't know if you've seen my latest novel. It's titled, *Screaming Bloody Murder*. My previous books have become best sellers around the world, but this one was just released last month. Keningham Press," she beamed.

Neil stood stiffly leaning away from her. "I'm sorry, but who are you?"

Marla cuffed him lightly on the arm. "You're funny! I know your sense of humor from your work. Brilliant, really brilliant. I'm Marla Page, of course."

Jack Burns held out a protective arm in front of his friend. "Marla, Neil isn't here to join our group, and he can't be expected to have read your books. He only stopped by to say hello, and decided to ride along on the tram tour."

Neil smiled apologetically. "Right. Sorry I don't know your work, but I appreciate that you're a fan.

Maybe I'll have a chance to read one of your books, too, Ms. …"

"*Page. Marla Page.*" Her tone was icy. "I'll get a copy of my latest thriller to you. It got a rave review in the *Tribune*."

She spun on her heel and stalked off, knocking into Grace and Frances who were holding Benny and Trixie. "Must you two take those idiotic toys with you wherever you go?!" Her eyes were blazing.

Grace glared indignantly. "Not that it's any of your business, but Benny has many readers who would be disappointed not to see him."

Marla's eyes narrowed. "Can't you see that you make us all look ridiculous? That fur ball is a goddamn puppet! He can't think. He can't speak." She rounded on Frances. "And that doll looks like the spawn of Satan."

"How dare you!" Frances hissed, her face dark. "You write stories about sickos who perform perverse acts on decent people and you criticize *us* who teach morality lessons to children? You have no concept of the kind of wholesome literature that most people want to read."

Alex stepped in between them. "All right, ladies. I think we're getting a little carried away here. You all write well for different readers. Let's just leave it at that. Anyway, it's about time to go outside to meet the tram. Hope you all like the tour."

She turned away, clenching her fists, and chewing on her lower lip. Noticing that Jack, Matthew, and Neil LeRoy had witnessed the scene, she walked over to them, to try to play down the hostility.

Holding out her hand to Neil she said, "I'm Alex Trotter, the tour operator, Mr. LeRoy. I know everyone here is happy to see you, and please feel free to join us any time you want. I wasn't sure who you were until Marla called out your name. But I certainly know your reputation as a best-selling author; although I have to confess that I haven't read any of your books."

"Oh. Well, that's honest, anyway," the author shrugged. "I hope you will. Anyway, I've got my thirty dollars here for the tram if there's room. I've been meaning to take that tour, so thought I'd tag along and catch up with my old friend." He patted Jack on the shoulder before reaching into his back pocket and taking two bills out of his wallet.

Alex accepted the money. "Thanks. No problem. We don't need the whole tram to ourselves, anyway. I only arranged to have it stop here, and asked them to point out all the writers' homes on this run. Many are private residences now, so you'd never know. There's lots more of interest, of course."

"It's a place with a storied past," Neil offered.

"Yes, it is. Well, I need to make sure the others are all here and ready to go. We'll be boarding in about five minutes. See you shortly."

***

TEN MINUTES LATER the open-air tram was proceeding up Whitehead Street until it came to a stop in front of the Spanish colonial villa at number 907. "You all probably know whose house this is," Brian, the guide said into his mic, continuing his lively narration. "This is where Ernest Hemingway and his wife Pauline lived from 1931 to 1939, and where he wrote several of his classics in the second-floor studio in the attached building. It's open to the public now as a museum.

"Two other interesting features of the house are its swimming pool, that was the first one built in Key West, and the 50 six-toed cats that live here that are said to be descendants of a Maine Coon that was given to Hemingway by a sea captain friend. They all have names and are allowed to go wherever they please on the property. You may know that Hemingway loved cats for their curiosity and independence.

"We'll be passing by the homes of other famous writers who lived here, like Tennessee Williams, Robert Frost, Philip Caputo, and the poet, Page Merrill, but they're all private residences now and not open to the public.

"Our next stop will be the Bahamian Village, a twelve-block area that was the site of the first settlers from the Bahamas in the 19th century. Europeans who immigrated to the Bahamas from America became known as Conchs, named for what they liked to eat. Later, all Bahamians who came to Key West were called Conchs, and eventually, all residents of the Florida Keys became known as Conchs.

"That leads me to the story of the Conch Republic, which is where you are, if you didn't know. We actually seceded from the United States back in 1982 when the Border Patrol set up a blockade on U.S. 1, just north of the Keys. They'd stop us to make us prove that we were citizens of the United States, to be allowed to drive onto the mainland.

"When Key West Mayor Dennis Wardlow couldn't get a court injunction in Miami to stop the blockade, the next day, April 23, he read the Proclamation of Secession from the Union on Mallory Square, and declared that the Conch Republic was a separate and independent nation.

"After a minute of rebellion, the now *Prime Minister* Wardlow surrendered to the Admiral in charge of the Key West Naval Base and demanded one billion dollars in foreign aid for reparations to rebuild our nation after the siege." He paused for the laughter and wise cracks to abate before continuing.

"We take it very seriously, folks. Well, as seriously as we take anything. By an Act of Congress all residents of the Keys hold dual citizenships as both Conchs and Americans. We have our own flag bearing our logo that's a conch shell at its center, under which is our motto, 'We Seceded Where Others Failed.'" There were more chuckles.

"That's right. We have our own ambassador and diplomats, and we issue passports that have been accepted in thirteen countries in the Caribbean as well as in several countries in Europe."

***

THE TOUR CONTINUED for another hour, going past such attractions as the Truman Little White House, Smother's Beach, Mallory Square, and ending at Hemingway's favorite bar, Sloppy Joe's.

As they were coming back to the C'est la Vie, Alex glanced around at her group. They seemed to have enjoyed the tour, and were in a good mood. Hopefully, that would continue into the evening when they would be eating together in the hotel's dining room, followed by a visit to the nightclub next door.

Monday evening

Chapter 9

"ISN'T THIS A LOVELY SETTING?" Flossie Quill asked of the other five authors at her table.

Cynthia Hart was straightening her silverware and unfolding her napkin. Looking around, appreciatively, with a dreamy look on her face, she responded, "I think there's nothing more comforting than an English tearoom. It's the perfect symbol of shelter from the cold and dark, to be served soothing hot tea and sweets."

Marla Page turned a jaundiced eye on her. "Thank you, Miss Marple. If you hadn't noticed, this isn't the Bertram's Hotel, it's 85 degrees out, and it's sunny. And who wants tea? I just want a stiff drink."

Jack Burns raised his water glass. "I'll second that. And why are we here for dinner while the sun's still up, anyway?"

Adeline Bloom made tsk! tsk! sounds. "We had to eat early because we didn't have a proper lunch. I noticed that there was a bar off the lobby, so I'm sure you'll get more than your share of libations – if you haven't already."

"Madam, I've only been here for five hours. Give me a chance."

Matthew Evans nervously tapped his fingers on the table. "Uh, I think Flossie and Cynthia make a fair point. There's an undeniable coziness about the place, and it's nice and quiet. We'll probably get enough noise and excitement at 'Some Like it Hot,' and any other clubs we check out."

A pretty dark-haired waitress with tawny skin approached, carrying menus. Her short black skirt showed off her long, well-shaped legs.

Jack came to attention, swiveling around to look over her over from head to foot. "Well, things are looking up, in more ways than one! Here we have a lovely Senorita to take care of us. Tell me, my dear, are you Cuban or Bahamian?"

The girl modestly lowered her eyes. "My family is from Jamaica, but I've lived here since I was a child." Her voice had the unmistakable lilt of her native island country.

"I'm sorry if you've had to wait," she continued, looking at the others. "My name is Selena and I'm at your service. Do you know what you would like to drink?"

"Now you're talking my language," Jack enthused. "I'll have a Stoli on the rocks, honey. And not too many rocks," he added, with a wink.

Selena stiffened a little. "I'm sorry, sir, but we don't have Stolichnaya vodka. Is Absolut all right?"

"Absolutely," Jack grinned.

The waitress seemed relieved to shift her attention to the others who ordered, in turn: a tall rum drink for Marla, wine for Matthew, while the other three women stayed with water.

***

At the other authors' table, Virgil Meade was making a toast for the occasion. "I raise my glass to all of us. Tomorrow we begin a new chapter of the Oak Park Authors League. Not only will we have verbal intercourse with more monetarily successful wordsmiths, but we will have a spotlight shone upon us to brighten our own futures."

Joan O'Leary turned to Alex. "I think he's saying that publishers and media people will be there looking for new talent."

Grace Tuttle brightened, displaying her Chiclet-sized front teeth. "I've heard there are some Disney people here. Just think, Walt Disney started with a mouse named Steamboat Willie and created an empire and made a fortune." Holding up Benny she cooed, "You could be the next Disney star, baby. With your looks and my stories, we could be rich!"

Alex studied the beaver puppet. "Isn't Benny commercially made? You can't get a copyright for him, can you?"

Grace's eyes narrowed. "You get a copyright on something that's *written*. You're talking about a trademark, but Benny is a unique character. There is only one Benny Beaver in Grace Tuttle books, and the books all have copyrights. You can't separate out Benny from my stories."

Alex didn't want to argue with the woman. They were supposed to be having a cordial, relaxing dinner, and the conversation appeared to be going off into a ditch. "Okay. I'm glad you're confident in that. I was just wondering. That's all."

Ethan O'Leary appeared to be troubled. Looking intently at Benny, he turned towards Grace. "Uh, Ms. Tuttle, I'm not positive, but to me that puppet looks like Bucky Beaver that was the Ipana toothpaste character for years. If I'm right, you should know that Bucky was created by Walt Disney in the 1950s. I'd be careful displaying that puppet around them, if that's the case. The drawings in your book are pretty generic, but the puppet is another matter."

Grace's small dark eyes became pinpoints and her upper lip rose above her large front teeth into a snarl. "Look, Mr. O'Leary, in your science fiction you can make up an entirely different universe. Those of us who write about the real world have to use what's already here. And there's 'nothing new under the sun,' as Solomon said three thousand years ago."

"I'm just telling you for your own good —"

"Grace's right," Frances Primm interjected. "I didn't make Trixie, either. She had a tag, too, from the toy maker. She was 'Molly,' as I remember, but I gave her a new identity. Do you think I have to share my royalties with Mattel because I bought their doll? I don't think writers are responsible to create anything other than ideas with their words. Not physical objects in their stories."

Ethan held up his hands. "Hey, I'm not a patent or trademark attorney. Obviously. I'm just saying, if Grace talks to Disney, it might be a good idea if she doesn't try to sell them on her books using her hand puppet. He might be their creation, and protected by their trademark.

"And, by the way, it's not easy to avoid using someone else's concept about outer space. There's a lot of science fiction material out there. When I send in a manuscript to the Copyright office, I'm always worried that something I've written has been used before. And they don't give a damn if it's unintentional."

Alex's mind was spinning, trying to come up with another subject that wasn't controversial. *How about those Bears?* Definitely not. These people weren't sports fans.

Her thoughts were interrupted just then as she became surrounded by a cloud of floral perfume. Looking up, she saw several heavily made up, bewigged women in sequined costumes. strutting by in high platform heels.

"Here we are girls," the leader, a mocha-colored beauty, trilled in a falsetto voice. "A lovely table by the window for the five of us."

The dining room had gone silent as everyone's attention became focused on the flamboyant new arrivals. The dark-skinned member of the group made a show of rearranging a feather boa over a mini skirt, and crossing shapely calves and thighs encased in fishnet hosiery.

Frances's fork clattered on her salad plate as she stared, slack-jawed. "Oh, my God! Who are those crazy-looking people?"

Alex calmly answered, "I assume they're female impersonators from 'Some Like it Hot.' The visiting performers often stay here. I don't know why they're in stage make-up and dress this early, though. They must have had a matinee show, in addition to having a show tonight."

Virgil Meade jutted out his chin and stared off into space. "'All the world's a stage," he emoted, "and all the men and women merely players: they have their exits and their entrances; and one man in his time plays many parts, his acts being seven ages.' William Shakespeare." He lowered his head and closed his eyes.

Joan shared a meaningful glance with Alex who was the first one to break the awkward silence that followed. "Yes, well, I suppose that's true, but I know that the impersonators don't usually spend their days in drag. In fact, they're almost unrecognizable when they're not made up. They look like ordinary guys."

Joan chimed in. "I think it's fascinating how they can transform themselves to look and even sound like women. I've heard one sing like Barbra Streisand."

"Fascinating?!" Grace countered, incredulously. "There's nothing 'fascinating' about men who deny their sexual identity. Perverse, is what it is. What talent does it take to glob on mascara and lipstick and parade around in bouffant wigs? I don't wear any make-up or get my hair done, and I look better than they do."

There was another uncomfortable silence as everyone carefully avoided looking at the speaker's dull complexion, small dark eyes, and rabbit overbite.

After a few moments, Alex cleared her throat and said slowly, "I understand that female impersonators are unusual and take a little getting used to, but I hope you'll all join me in taking in their act tonight. I should warn you that the humor can get a little raunchy −"

"See?" Frances jumped in, supporting her friend. "There's nothing funny about 'raunchy,' either.

Alex exhaled slowly, clenching her napkin. "I just think you should attend one show to see what it's like since you haven't seen female impersonators before. These people are talented singers, dancers, and some tell jokes. You might find that you enjoy the show. If you don't like it, you can leave, of course. Fair enough?" She looked around the table for a response.

Ethan turned to his wife with raised eyebrows. She nodded in response to his silent question. "Joan and I want to go. Those are professional performers, after all, and they've been hired by a popular nightclub. They must be good."

Virgil nodded somberly. "I believe it's a form of legitimate theatre deserving of our attention and appreciation."

"So that's a 'yes'?" Alex teased. "How about you two ladies?" She looked expectantly at Grace and Frances.

"I'll try it if you will," Frances challenged her as a dare.

Grace wrinkled her nose. "Oh, all right. I guess it won't kill me to see it once."

Alex breathed a sigh of relief. "Okay, then. We'll all go. And I trust that none of you will regret it," she added, feeling suddenly apprehensive.

Monday night

Chapter 10

THE BLUE-LIT NIGHTCLUB was wall-to-wall people when Alex's party walked inside. Amplified salsa music made normal conversation impossible, but patrons seemed content to stand around moving in time to the beat and sipping their drinks.

Alex could feel the bass notes vibrate down to her toes as she looked around for the manager. Identifying him as the man who had a badge pinned on his tuxedo, with shoulder-length blond hair, she elbowed her way over to him. Once there, she had to shout at him to be heard. Nodding that he understood her, he consulted a card, and pointed towards the stage.

Wriggling her way back to her clients, she motioned for them to follow her as she disappeared back into the crowd. Breaking through to a small clearing, she stopped and waited for them to catch up. When they did, she called out, "We're going down to the second tier. We have tables 8, 9 and 10." They all nodded or made an OK sign.

Walking in single file, they descended the concrete stairs that ran alongside the café tables. Arriving on the second tier, they picked their way across, stepping over people and mouthing "excuse me" until they came to their three tables. In the tight space, everyone took the first chair they came to, and sat down.

It occurred to Alex that it would have been prudent to have visited the restrooms before they became so confined. Taking a quick head count, she saw that four of them must have done just that – or were lost. At any rate, it would be pointless to go back now and check since there were so many people milling around. She'd wait until more people were seated, if the others hadn't joined them by then.

Noticing her anxiety, Flossie patted her hand and smiled encouragement. "Don't worry, dear. They're all adults. They'll find us, or they'll find another place to sit. I think you should just relax. This is such a colorful place, isn't it?" She commented as she looked around at posters of men in drag on the lavender walls."

"Oh, it's that all right," Alex responded, thinking that some in her group probably found it more gaudy and obscene than colorful. "Let's just hope the acts are good."

Flossie nodded, knowingly. "We're all adults when it comes to entertainment, too. Even Frances and Grace have heard some bad language and off-color jokes. You don't have to protect everyone's sensibilities."

Alex's eyes widened with pleasure. This woman always said just the right thing at the right time. "Thank you, Flossie. That *is* what I was worried about. But you're right. I'm not in control of everything. Oh, here comes the waitress to take our drink order. Let's get something tall and cool."

"For my money, that would be Matthew Evans," Flossie said, winking. "I'm still waiting for you two to get together, you know." Alex shook her head and made a face in mock exasperation.

Just as their rum drinks arrived, the lights blinked, signaling that the show would soon start. Alex glanced down their row and saw that everyone was there now, except for Jack Burns. Looking around, she spotted him at the bar nuzzling a woman she had never seen before, which was undoubtedly true for Jack as well. *Oh, well, as long as everyone is enjoying themselves...* she thought.

She just wished that Grace had taken Benny back to her room before they came to the club. Probably out of habit, the woman had slipped the puppet on her hand and was absently petting its nylon fur.

The band started playing some rousing music, ending with a crash of cymbals. People quieted down and looked up at the stage expectantly. The shimmering curtain parted and was slowly pulled back to reveal a Marilyn Monroe look-alike in a white halter dress, attempting to hold down her skirt that was being blown up by a floor fan. The audience cheered and hooted in appreciation of the impersonator's recreation of the iconic scene.

"Ooh, this tickles," 'Marilyn' giggled. Then, speaking breathily into the standing mic, she cooed, "Welcome to 'Some Like It Hot.' I'll be your mistress tonight. I mean, your mistress *of ceremonies* tonight, to introduce our sexy and talented ladies.

"And our first lady of the evening is a comedienne who comes to us from South Beach. That's in Miami." She fluttered her eyelashes coyly as the crowd laughed. "Why don't you join me in giving a warm welcome to…Miss…Fonda…Dix!" Hoots and catcalls followed as the dark-skinned performer emerged from behind the curtain.

Alex recognized him from the hotel dining room, although he was now dressed in a slinky gold gown with a skirt split up the center. On his head was an outrageous red bouffant wig. As he sashayed out onto the stage, he seductively twirled a black feather boa before slowly drawing it across his bodice.

"Good evening, good evening, my darlings," he trilled, fluttering his hands in response to the cheering. "And thank you, Marilyn, for that introduction." He flashed a broad smile at the sex symbol before she turned and walked to the back of the stage, swiveling her hips.

Turning to the audience, he spoke in a stage whisper into the mic. "Sweet girl, Marilyn. But I'm afraid she's not too bright." He glanced back, as though making sure she was gone. "She went to the doctor the other day complaining that she hurt 'everywhere.' The doctor said, 'That's impossible. Show me where. Marilyn took her finger and pressed it against her breast and cried out, 'Ouch!' Then she pressed her finger on her arm and cried 'Ouch!' again. When she pressed it on her leg she said, 'Ouch!' for a third time. The doctor sat back for a moment, considering, before he said, 'Well, I have good news for you. You have a broken finger.'" The punch line was greeted with gales of laughter.

Fonda Dix continued. "Yesterday I said to her, 'I heard your birthday is January 10. What year?' She responded, 'Oh, it's the same every year.'" Another wave of laughter followed.

"Thank you, darlings. You seem to be a good audience. Believe me, it's tough getting up every night telling jokes. I remember when people laughed when I told them I'd be a comedian. Well, they're not laughing now.

"Anyway, let me see who's here tonight. Looks like an attractive group. You should have seen the women who were here last night. Oh, my God, they couldn't get a date off a calendar.

"How many of you men are here with your wife?" Hands went up. "Okay. How many men are here with someone else's wife? Ah, more hands. You, sir, raised your hand twice. That's a nice arrangement." The crowd roared, getting into the act.

"Run a spotlight over the audience, Joe. Thanks, sweetie." Fonda suddenly stopped and stared. "Wait a minute. I can't believe it. There's a woman over there on the second tier showing her beaver." There was a collective gasp as everyone stared at the spotlit table. Alex felt her blood go cold. She looked over at Grace who was frozen.

The comedian stepped off the stage and hopped up to Grace's table in a flash. "Do you mind if I put my hand up your beaver?" he asked the unresponsive Grace as the audience howled. "This is what I've always wanted. Why haven't I thought of this?" He fondled the puppet.

Alex stood, but Flossie put out her hand. "You'll only make it worse, dear," she cautioned.

Fonda Dix was still going strong. "Did you get your beaver here, in Key West? Or did you bring it with you?" The audience was laughing hysterically now. Grace hadn't moved a muscle or made eye contact with the comedian. Frances, however, was staring daggers at him.

"Well, darling, thanks for letting me stroke your beaver, but I'd better go back on stage. I just want to thank you for giving me a great idea for my act. Let's give her a hand, folks. She's been a good sport, although I still don't know why she pulled out her beaver for all of us to see." The audience clapped and cheered.

As soon as the spotlight was taken off Grace's table, Alex jumped up and raced over to her. "C'mon Grace, let's get out of here. I'm so sorry about this. I had no idea that we'd be subjected to this."

"*We* weren't subjected to this. *I* was," Grace spat, her face red with rage. "And I'm not going to forget this. I'm a decent, God-fearing woman, and I won't take this humiliation lying down."

Chapter 11

ALEX HUSTLED GRACE TO THE BACK of the lounge as the others followed, most of them reluctantly. As they neared the bar, Alex caught the eye of Jack Burns, who raised his drink in greeting, before he staggered towards them with one arm draped heavily over his young female companion.

Ignoring the disapproving glares, he smiled crookedly and took an ungainly bow, causing his glass to tip, spilling out some of his drink. "I'd like you all to meet my friend, Lola. A lovely girl…and she reads."

"Oh, how *nice*," Flossie responded with forced enthusiasm. "What do you read, my dear?"

The platinum blonde's forehead became creased in confusion. "Uh, well, I'm not sure what you mean. I guess I can read most words. I read well enough to get my GED, anyway. That makes me a high school graduate, y'know," she added, beaming.

"Looks like you've got a real winner there, Jack," Marla acidly intoned.

Lola stuck out her lower lip and lowered her false eyelashes, doubting that she hadn't been complimented.

Jack gave her a squeeze. "Don't mind Marla, darlin'. She's jes jealous that you have looks and personality." His eyes dropped down to the top of her half-exposed breasts. "And big titties."

Frances hrumphed in disgust. "How much vulgarity do we have to put up with in one evening? And now from a man who's drunk as a skunk."

Jack threw back his head and laughed. "Thank you for the perfect opening to quote Winston Churchill: 'I may be drunk Madam, but you're ugly. And in the morning I'll be sober, but you'll still be ugly.'"

Frances grabbed Jack's shirtfront, twisting it into a wad. "Look here, none of us needs to be insulted by the likes of you…you boozing womanizer."

"Unhand me, woman, unless you want more of me." He raised an eyebrow in Groucho Marx style.

Alex noticed that people in the last row were turning around to shush them, so got between Jack and Frances. "Okay, I don't think any of this is helpful. We're only making a bad situation worse, and saying things we'll regret in the morning. There's no reason to turn on each other."

Lola dropped Jack's arm and moved in close to Frances, studying her face. "Have you ever thought about wearing makeup? I could help you with that. I work in a salon in town. We could make your eyes look bigger, and give you a little color. You do have small pores, so could give you even coverage."

Frances's mouth fell open.

Oblivious to the woman's reaction, Lola turned to the other women. "Everybody needs a little help to look their best. I think you'd all enjoy seeing what a difference the right makeup can do for you. We carry the best products that aren't animal tested or anything."

Alex felt like she had lost all control. "Uh, thanks, Lola, but I don't think —"

Lola's face became animated, "Oh, I know what you're going to say. *You* need help with your hair. You're very pretty, otherwise. Sorry, I forgot to mention that we're connected to a hair salon. They could work wonders on you, too."

Jack patted Lola on the head. "See? I told you she was nice."

Grace clenched her jaw, her breath coming in pants. "We don't need insults from either of you. After what I had to put up with from that creature on the stage…"

Jack laid a hand on her shoulder. "Listen, that was shitty, what that comedian did to you. I mean, you're weird as hell, but that crossed a line, even for me. And that guy shouldn't get away with it. Believe me, I could put that ass-hole in a world of hurt." He made a fist and pounded it into the palm of his other hand. "I could break that faggot like a pretzel."

Alex pulled him back. "All right! That's quite enough." You all need to get an early start tomorrow to set up your tables at the seminar, right? Maybe we should call it a night. I'm sorrier than I can say that things turned out as they did. All I can say is that I'll try to avoid problems in the future."

Just then a clear soprano voice was heard coming from the stage. "Oh, my man I love him so … He'll never know. All my life is just despair … but I don't care …"

"Listen, Ethan," Joan said, tugging at his sleeve. "It's a Barbra Streisand impersonator. Let's go sit down and watch him."

81

"Joan–that *is* Barbra Streisand's voice. The guy's lip-syncing."

Marla drew closer. "Whatever. I'll go with you. I don't give a fuck if he's playing a radio. It's still early. No sense having the evening spoiled for all of us with this nonsense."

Adeline Bloom looked questioningly at Cynthia and Flossie. "What do you girls think? I could go either way, but I'd like to stay."

The voice swelled on the second verse, "Oh, my man, I love him so!" it now insisted, filling the theatre.

Flossie looked longingly at the stage. "Oh, I think we should see the show through. This could be our only opportunity to see something like this."

"That's fine," Alex said. "Anyone who wants to hear the rest of the show, should stay. Anyone who wants to go back to the hotel, should feel free to go.

"What about you, Virgil?" The author appeared to have not heard as he stared off into space. "Virgil?"

"Oh, yes. I was just thinking of 'despair,' that's in the song lyric. Walt Whitman wrote a poem about despair. If you will allow me…

'Despairing cries float ceaselessly toward me,
Day and night,
The sad voice of Death -- the call of my nearest lover, putting forth,
alarmed, uncertain,
This sea I am quickly to sail, come tell me,
Come tell me where I am speeding--tell me my destination.'

Alex sighed deeply. "Well, that's cheerful. Does that mean you want to stay?

"That would be an affirmative, Ms. Trotter."

Jack Burns chuckled. "See? We all need to live now, while we can. And my 'nearest lover' is alive and well." He planted a noisy kiss on Lola's cheek.

Matthew leaned over and whispered to Alex. "You want me to try to get Jack back to the hotel, now?"

"I think Lola will take care of that," she murmured.

Addressing the rest of the group she said, "So we'll go our own ways, then. I'll see most of you in the dining room for breakfast. They serve between seven and nine-thirty. Good night, everybody."

Alex started towards the exit as Matthew caught up with her to hold open the door. "You've had quite a first day. Let me say that you came through it admirably. It got pretty dicey in there and you diffused the situation very effectively."

"Thanks, but I'm also the one who planned the evening that turned out to be so dicey."

Matthew smirked. "And I was the one who promised you we'd all get along in Key West." He shrugged. "We can't beat ourselves up. Anyway, I was just thinking that we haven't had that talk about the Art Institute and our stalled art careers. Do you feel up to that now? We could stop at the hotel bar for a drink. What do you say?"

Alex paused for only a moment. "I think that's just what I'd like, Matthew. Let's go."

Tuesday morning

Chapter 12

EARLY THE NEXT MORNING, Alex was jarred into consciousness by a ringing telephone. Only half-awake, she seized the receiver to hear a mechanical voice announce that it was seven o'clock. Still disoriented, she peered out from under her sheet and looked around the room, bringing her back to reality. *Oh, yeah. Key West. How could I forget?*

Her mind went back to last night, which gave her a sinking feeling, even as her dull headache reminded her that she had had too much to drink. She recalled ending the evening having a last mango mojito with Matthew Evans. Other than that, what had happened? Oh, right. Grace Tuttle had been mocked and humiliated by the comedian at 'Some Like It Hot,' Jack Burns had gotten drunk and insulted Frances, and his 'friend' Lola had chimed in, offering unappreciated makeover advice to Frances, and every other woman there.

It had not been her best day as a tour operator.

Although, she had to admit that she had enjoyed having a late drink with Matthew, and trading stories about life at the Art Institute. He had shown a talent for mimicking the eccentric teachers they had both studied under; and she had amused him with her stories, including how she used to shift her chair in figure drawing classes to avoid certain frontal views of the nude models.

When he showed her examples of his graphic art on his IPad, she saw how talented he was. He shouldn't have a problem getting work as an illustrator, or cover designer, from even the best-selling authors at the seminar.

She did feel a pang of guilt that she probably wouldn't be telling Arlie about that part of her evening. Not that there was anything wrong with her having a drink with one of her clients. And she and Arlie didn't have an 'understanding' that would make such a casual get-together off-limits, either. Or did they?

After getting out of bed, she showered quickly, dressed in a turquoise print skirt and white sleeveless top, and started down for breakfast.

The dining room was so crowded that she had to look around to find someone from her group. Spotting Flossie Quill sitting with Cynthia Hart and Adeline Bloom, she headed over to join them.

"Oh, hi, dear," Flossie said, pulling back a chair for her. "Please join us. We haven't even ordered yet."

As she sat down and unrolled her napkin, and took out her silverware, Flossie kept staring and smiling at her like a Cheshire cat.

Alex glanced over. "What?"

"Oh, I was just wondering… I saw you leave the club with Matthew last night. Did you two have a nice time together?"

Cynthia and Adeline put down their coffee cups, and looked at Alex expectantly.

In response, she shrugged and raised her palms, saying, "We just had a drink together and talked about our shared experiences in art school. It was very pleasant, but that's all there was to it. I hate to disappoint all of you that there wasn't any mad passion. Now, what's for breakfast?" She reached for a menu.

Flossie's face fell. "Well, it's a start. By the way, they also have a buffet table over there with sweet breads, juices, and coffee, if that's all you want. I can tell you that the banana bread is delicious."

Alex looked up. "Thanks, but I think I need something more substantial. I had a few too many mango mojitos last night, I'm afraid. Have you seen anyone else from our group?" She glanced around.

Adeline leaned forward, her 'author' ribbon grazing the table. "Not yet. But look two tables over. Do you know who that is?" she asked in an excited whisper.

Alex slyly shifted her gaze to where Adeline indicated. The only person at that table was a handsome light-colored black man with dreadlocks wearing a white tunic top. He was calmly eating a plate of scrambled eggs. "Oh. Is that…what's his name…'Fonda Dix'?"

"Yes!" Adeline could barely contain her excitement. "We're expecting Grace and Frances to come down any minute. They're on the first shift at our tables. What do you think Grace will do when she sees him?"

Alex grimaced. "Well, don't worry. I'm sure that Grace wants to put last night behind her and just ignore him. I know I do. She might not even recognize him. I don't think I would have if you hadn't called my attention to him. Let's just not point him out to her, okay?"

"Oh, right. Right." Adeline agreed, nodding emphatically. Just then she looked up and smiled broadly. "Oh, look who's here!" Her eyes darted back to Alex. "It's Grace and Frances! We were just saying that you two should be coming along as you're on the early shift. Weren't we Alex?"

"Yes. Yes we were. Have a seat. I just got here, too, and no one's ordered yet, so you're right on time." She glanced up. "And here comes the waitress."

While they waited for their meals, Alex tried to keep everyone's attention focused on one another by asking about the seminar lectures scheduled for that day.

Flossie clasped her hands in anticipation. "I'm going to go hear Alyssa Stone on 'The Heart of the Romance Novel.' Isn't that a cute title? She's wonderful at creating believable heroes and heroines; always coming up with an unusual personal flaw, and a baffling predicament, that the characters overcome by the end of the book."

Cynthia made a little moue. "I'll have to miss that one cuz I want to hear about 'The Year's Ten Best Books,' to see what makes them so special in the eyes of the judges, whether they're romances, or whatever."

Grace propped Benny up on her lap, placing his paws on the table. "*We're* going to make ourselves available for the *Disney* people," she sniffed. "This may be our only opportunity to be discovered. I know we're just what they're looking for." She patted Benny's head.

Leaning in, she confided, "They had to go back to Hans Christian Anderson's '*Snow Queen*' for the idea for '*Frozen.*' Shows you how desperate they are –

they've run out of princesses. Little girls don't look for a man to give their lives meaning anymore, anyway."

"Just a minute," Adeline snapped. "Women will always find a special happiness with a kind, loving man."

"Yeah, like all of us have," Frances said sourly. "Trixie is the ideal female. She's full of life with an independent spirit and a vivid imagination."

Alex glanced over at the doll to see if the creature looked pleased with the compliments. Thinking its mouth turned up, she about choked on her coffee.

"Are you okay, dear?" Flossie asked.

"Ack! Yes, I'm fine." Alex drank some water to clear her throat and calm her nerves. "I was about to say that I'd like to attend a couple of the talks myself, but I was thinking I could help out selling at your tables if most of you want to attend talks that are scheduled at the same time."

Flossie patted her arm. "Oh, that's nice of you, but we should be able to work it out among the ten of us. I can't think that we need more than two people to hold down the fort at any one time."

"I doubt that we can count on Jack to take his turn," Grace scoffed. "Probably won't get up til noon – and then he won't be alone."

"Let's just take care of our own business," Flossie advised, not unkindly.

"That's enough for me with all that's going on," Cynthia agreed.

"From what I saw on the schedule, the seminars should be finished by four o'clock," Alex noted. "I'd like to arrange for an outing after that. Does a tour of the Hemingway house sound good? Or a boat ride?"

"Either one for me," Adeline answered.

"I can't say what I want to do several hours from now," Frances groused.

"All right, fine," Alex said calmly. "I'll stop by your table during the afternoon and see how everyone feels. Maybe no one will want to do anything after the first day."

Looking at Adeline, Alex became alarmed to see the woman's face turn ashen and her eyes widen in shock as she stared up at something.

"What is it, Adeline?" Alex asked, turning to see the man they knew as Fonda Dix bearing down on their table.

"Good morning, ladies," the performer trilled, extending his hands out of flowing sleeves. "I'm so pleased to see my friend here." He placed his hands on Grace's shoulders that became rigid under his touch as her face reddened. He laughed, manically. "Actually, I mean *this* friend." He picked up Benny, petting him.

Grace snatched the puppet back, clutching it to her chest.

Alex was the first to find her voice. "I'm sorry, Mr., er, 'Dix,' but we don't really welcome your company. In fact, we were all offended at your using Grace and her puppet as objects of mockery in your act, so please leave us. Thank you." She picked up her coffee cup as a prop to hide her discomfort.

Fonda Dix still appeared to be amused as he remained standing there grinning. Glancing around the table, he said in a saccharine voice, "Well, as a comedian I'm sorry that you didn't see the humor. But I'll be happy to leave you alone. I just came over to tell 'Mrs. Beaver' something."

He bent over and whispered in Grace's ear. As he talked, her eyes began to bulge out and her lips tightened into a thin line.

Tuesday afternoon

Chapter 13

ALEX ARRIVED AT THE yellow painted San Carlos Institute just before noon. She had spent most of the morning doing some exploratory sightseeing and making phone calls.

Glancing up to admire the ornamental façade, she mounted the shallow steps and opened the door. Inside, the building's Cuban roots were reflected in the black and white tiled floors and Moorish arches. Prominently positioned in the atrium space, was the statue of Jose Marti, his arm raised defiantly as he led his rebel forces to free Cuba from Spanish rule.

Alex had been in the landmark building only once before, with a small group of tourists. Now, it was bustling with people who were circulating among the rooms to buy books, or sitting on the red plush seats in the auditorium listening to a lecture, or lined up outside the library to have one of their favorite writers sign a copy of his or her latest best-seller.

Alex had arrived early for her seminar that was being given by a popular mystery writer who had been a forensic toxicologist. It was not only a subject she was interested in, but it would be something she could share with Arlie that would interest him too.

But first, she'd have to find the OPAL tables to see how things were going. *At least to make sure they haven't killed one another*, she thought glumly. She crossed the lobby and peered into the next room.

Looking around the exhibit hall, she caught sight of Virgil Meade holding forth with some lady who was slowly backing away from him.

Alex waved to get Virgil's attention, and started over towards him.

When she walked up, he clapped his hands in greeting. "Oh, Miss Trotter! I was just regaling Miss Peters here with some poetic imagery to help her get started on the road to writing rhythmic verse."

Alex smiled at the woman who looked pleadingly back at her.

Virgil's mind seemed to be on something else as he stared off into space, his brow furrowed. Shifting his attention back to the two women, he explained, "I was just trying to bring together a convergence that occurred to me when I said that Miss Peters was looking 'down the road' to writing. To Miss Peters, he said, "Miss Trotter is our group's travel agent who tries to find the 'road less travelled by that will make all the difference,' as Robert Frost wrote.

He chuckled to himself. "Well, that's the mind of a writer for you. Word images. Connections."

Alex cleared her throat. "Yes, you do enjoy words, Virgil, especially your own. I need to get going to a lecture. I just wanted to see how the group is doing. Why don't you show me to your table? Do you mind if we excuse ourselves, Miss Peters?"

The woman shook her head, her eyes shining with gratitude. "Thank you. I mean, thank *you*, Mr. Meade, for your help. I'll work on what you told me." She turned and was gone in a flash.

Following Virgil, Alex soon saw the banner for the Oak Park Authors League that was on the wall over the tables set together at a right angle. Several of the members were in the area, some seated behind the tables, while others stood nearby.

Matthew, leaning against a wall, caught her eye and wiggled a few fingers at her. Alex did likewise and made her way over to him.

"Hi, Matthew. I'm actually here for a seminar," she glanced down at her watch, "but I wanted to check in with everyone. Is it going well?"

"Define 'well.'" He smiled crookedly. "We've all sold a few books and met some of our readers, which is always rewarding. We're just changing the guard, here. Actually, I'm off to a seminar, myself. 'Forensics Today in Mysteries' or some such thing."

"That's where *I'm* going."

"Great. Why don't you come with me."

"Sure. Just let me just say 'hello' to Flossie first, okay?"

"Fine. I'm supposed to be meeting Jack there, but I can't count on that. That was the plan last night. I ran into Neil LeRoy a little while ago, and he hadn't seen or heard from Jack yet today. Who knows? He could be off getting a facial from Lola."

"Oh, brother," Alex groaned.

Flossie crooked a finger at her to come over. "Oh, Alex! My goodness! You just missed the scout from Disney who came by and took Grace and Benny off somewhere. Can you believe it? Not five minutes ago. I saw the woman flash some sort of badge with a mouse on it, and heard her tell Grace that she knew her

92

'work.' She said there were, 'people who wanted to talk to her.'"

"Oh, my God, Flossie! Grace actually attracted the attention of someone from Disney!"

"I know. The woman looked very 'up-market,' if you know what I mean. Her hair was pulled back in a sleek chignon, and she wore these distinctive tortoise-shell frame square glasses. Her white pants suit looked like Vera Wang. It fit her like icing on a cake."

"Well, I can't wait to hear more about it, but I'm just on my way to a seminar on forensics in mysteries. Matthew's going too, coincidentally."

"Oh, my. Well, isn't this a providential day!"

Chapter 14

AT A QUARTER TO FOUR that afternoon, Alex was seated on one of the chintz sofas in the C'est La Vie lounge waiting for her group to come down. Earlier, they had reached an uneasy agreement to meet and walk over to Sloppy Joe's together to have a drink, and then head over to Mallory Square to watch the sun set.

Grace Tuttle had actually suggested the plan as a way of celebrating her good fortune: She had jubilantly spread the word that a Disney Studios' project manager named Lorna Green had approached her with the possibility of using Benny Beaver stories for an animated film.

In her state of euphoria, she hadn't even noticed that few of her fellow authors were very happy for her, much less wanted to go out and celebrate her good fortune. Most of them actively disliked her because she had always been so disagreeable and insulting in the past. And now they had cause to resent her, as well, for her enviable opportunity they considered to be undeserved.

Not only had her party idea been regarded as unseemly, since they weren't her friends, but particularly ill-chosen, as she had always disapproved of the consumption of alcohol for any reason.

Alex had taken the others aside to urge them to go along with Grace's wishes, thinking that the good cheer of the revelers in the bar and on Mallory Square would be infectious and ease tensions. Finally, they had all agreed to go along, mostly because they wanted to visit both places anyway, and wouldn't consider the get-together to be for Grace's benefit.

Flossie had been influential, arguing that it only seemed fair to try to make up to Grace for the humiliation she had suffered at the "Some Like It Hot" club the night before.

Frances had been of two minds, wanting to celebrate for Grace's sake, but not approving of alcohol, either. Apparently, she wanted to stay on Grace's 'good side,' as she confided to Alex, Grace might show Lorna Green her 'Trixie' books.

Marla Page had expressed disbelief that Disney people would even consider Grace's books as being up to their level. She thought it must be some kind of joke for some reason that she couldn't imagine.

Jack Burns had also scoffed at the idea of Grace's stories being used in a Disney film, enlightening Alex that only one percent of books are ever optioned for films, and of those, only one percent ever make it out of development. Grace would have many more hurdles to clear before she would see Benny on the screen.

Whatever their reasons, Alex was just relieved that they were all going. Her romanticized vision was that they would be put in a good mood in Hemingway's favorite bar, be swept up in the celebration on the plaza, and be inspired by watching the sunset over the Gulf. Of course, it was more likely that hatred, envy, and bitterness wouldn't be overcome by a party atmosphere for one evening.

To distract herself from her conflicting thoughts, she picked up a magazine and started flipping through it, glancing up whenever someone came through the lobby. Just as she started scanning an article entitled, "How to Find Peace and Harmony," her attention was diverted by a woman's crisp voice rapidly issuing instructions.

Looking up, Alex was startled to see that the speaker was a striking brunette in a white pants suit, wearing stylish glasses, just as Flossie had described the Disney representative, Lorna Green. A harried looking female assistant followed her, writing in a small notebook.

"Make half a dozen copies of all these forms, in case we want to go further with any of the authors we've talked to. And send the revised forms to both Legal and corporate, with a cover letter explaining my changes.

"Remember, we have a dinner meeting scheduled at seven with that journalist who was held prisoner by some jihadists in North Yemen, or some other God-forsaken place. Arrange for dinner to be served in one of the small conference rooms here at the hotel. Some kind of fresh fish, I think, for the entrée. Oh, and don't forget dessert. But not more Key lime pie, for God's sake– I don't want to be tortured too.

"All right? That should be it for tonight. We'll get an early start in the morning. I want to attend a couple of seminars, and I have more interviews. We'll have some downtime tomorrow night – dinner in the dining room by ourselves, and then I'd like to go to that night club next door. Have a few laughs. I heard the comedians are pretty raunchy, but funny. Just what I like.

"Then it's early to bed, and we'll hit the ground running the next day. Is that the last day? Honest to God, I need to check my phone for my schedule. How did people know where they were supposed to be, and what they were supposed to be doing, before wireless technology?"

Lorna Green was still giving orders as the two women went out the front door. Alex looked after them, shaking her head. Grace might be getting ahead of herself if she's so certain that Benny Beaver is going to be the latest Disney sensation. And, even if that is the case, she'll have to deal with that high-strung, demanding woman. Maybe it isn't such a great opportunity after all, particularly when you consider Jack's discouraging statistics.

As she turned back, she saw Grace coming into the lobby looking smug and self-assured as she held Benny aloft on her hand. Alex pasted a bright smile on her face and waved her over.

"Well, the guests of honor! You just missed that lady from Disney. Lorna Green. Isn't that her name?"

"W-w-what? Ms. Green was here looking for me, and you didn't tell her I'd be right down?"

Alex instantly regretted her ambiguous remarks. "No, I'm sorry, Grace. I didn't *speak* with Ms. Green. I just recognized her from Flossie's description. She's staying in the hotel, and I overheard her going over her schedule with her assistant."

Grace's small eyes bored into Alex with suspicion.

"That's all, Grace. She didn't say anything about you. She said that she was going to attend some seminars, and was meeting with a journalist; that kind of thing. Oh, and that she and her assistant were going to go to the nightclub next door tomorrow night for 'downtime' as she put it. As I've said, everyone who stays here ends up going there.'"

Grace lifted her upper lip, exposing her large front teeth. "I didn't know she was staying here," she grunted.

"Don't worry about that. I'm sure you won't be running into her all the time with so many people here for the seminar. Sounds like she has a full schedule to keep her busy, anyway."

Looking past Grace, Alex was relieved to see Frances, Adeline, Cynthia and Flossie, with the O'Learys and Virgil behind them. "Oh, look, here come the others to start celebrating your good fortune!"

Glancing back at Grace, she saw that the woman still had a sour look on her face. *Should be another fun-filled evening,* she thought dismally.

Tuesday evening

Chapter 15

ALEX STEERED GRACE towards the front door before anyone could become aware of the woman's foul mood. *What was wrong with her? Here, her books were being considered for a movie that would make her wealthy and famous, and now, she was in a snit, for no apparent reason.*

The others, who were confused at the hurried departure, voiced objections that not everyone was there, yet.

Alex called back over her shoulder, "They're meeting us at the bar. Let's just go."

Once outside, Alex pinched Grace's arm and hissed in her ear, "Try to look happy. These people are here to celebrate your lucky day."

Turning to the others, she said pleasantly, "Sloppy Joe's is only three blocks down, and Mallory Square is just two blocks beyond that."

Cynthia caught up to her. "Sloppy Joe was a friend of Hemingway's, right?"

Alex nodded and turned to include the others. "The owner of Sloppy Joe's in Hemingway's day was Joe Russell, who was one of his fishing and drinking buddies. But this bar we're going to isn't the original Sloppy Joe's. Hemingway was never in this bar."

Seeing their surprised expressions, she explained, "Years ago an owner of the original Sloppy Joe's had a dispute with the landlord and reopened the bar a few buildings down, on the corner of Greene Street and Duval. I hope that story doesn't spoil your visit for you. This Sloppy Joe's has the same appearance and spirit as the old place."

Ethan O'Leary shrugged his shoulders. "Hemingway's been gone for more than 50 years. I doubt that *any* place in town is much like it was when he was here."

"That's right," Flossie agreed. "Everything changes, but all of this puts us in mind of him and the other great writers who lived and wrote here." She made a broad gesture to include all of Duval Street.

"That's a good way to put it," Alex chimed in. "The Bohemian character of Key West that attracted writers and artists, hasn't changed. Anyway, let's get on to this Sloppy Joe's. I think Grace is ready to start celebrating, right Grace?"

Grace jutted out her jaw and squared her shoulders. "I'm more than ready. And nothing will spoil this occasion for me and Benny."

Frances put an arm around her. "Of course, nothing will spoil it. We're all happy for you."

***

THEY COULDN'T MISS SLOPPY JOE'S, since its name was painted in 3-foot tall block letters across both the front and the side of the building. And even from across the street they could hear the pounding beat and the wailing lyrics of classic rock music coming from within.

A hefty young bouncer, wearing an orange tee shirt, stood to the side of one of the front doors and nodded to the group as they filed past him.

Inside, there was a stage in back of the large open room where a country singer was performing his rendition of "Proud Mary," as he accompanied himself on the guitar, and a drummer kept the beat. A curved bar snaked along the entire side wall to accommodate a sizable number of people on stools, while other customers could sit at the simple wooden tables in the center of the room.

Alex looked around for the three others who were planning on meeting them there. Marla Page had said that she would be there after doing some shopping. Jack Burns and Matthew Evens had just said they'd be late. But after looking over the tables and the bar, and not seeing them, she suggested that they grab three tables and hold places for the late-comers.

As they did so, Alex showed Grace to a choice seat from which she could see the performers, and sat down next to her, while Frances sat across the table. The rest of the group took places at the other two tables, leaving three seats empty.

Within a couple of minutes, a waitress stopped by to ask for their drinks and appetizer orders. Alex said that she was treating Grace, and encouraged her to order whatever she'd like.

"I think I'll have a Margarita," Grace announced Frances said she'd have the same, and Alex made it three, and added an order of fresh fried shrimp.

After the waitress left, Grace turned to Alex. "What's a Margarita, anyway?"

Alex chuckled. "It's tequila, lime juice and Cointreau over ice, usually served in a wide shallow stemware glass with salt on the rim. Quite delicious. I think you'll like it, and it's a good time to have your first one. In fact, it's time that you had one, period."

Her attention became diverted by a woman who was laboriously making her way around tables with a large satchel, trying to keep it from knocking into things. "Oh, it's Marla." She waved her arms over her head to get Marla's attention.

Marla was breathing hard when she reached them. Alex remarked, "You must have been successful in your shopping trip."

"I did all right." Her answer was clipped and invited no further inquiries.

Alex gave a little shrug. "Well, good. You can sit here with us, or there are a couple other open seats. Suit yourself."

"I'll sit over there with the O'Learys." She lifted the case off the floor and lunged forward with it.

The waitress soon returned with the drinks and the shrimp appetizer for Alex's table. Grace eagerly picked up her glass with both hands and took a couple deep swallows. "Ooh, it's good. It's like lime-aid, right?"

Frances licked the edge of her glass before gulping some down, and smacking her lips. "It's very tasty."

Alex held up a cautionary hand. "Go easy, ladies. It takes a little time for the alcohol to hit you, but it will."

The singer on the stage broke into a catchy song, prompting Grace and Frances to bob their heads in time to the beat. Clinking their glasses, they took several more swigs of their drinks.

Alex let out a long sigh, and rested her chin on her hands. Looking around, she was pleased to see Jack Burns and Matthew Evans coming in. Closely behind them was Neil LeRoy. Standing up, she waved until Matthew saw her and nodded, holding up his index finger to say he'd be a moment.

After the men got their drinks, Jack led the way back to Alex's table, his eyes widening in shock when he saw what Grace and Frances were drinking.

"Well, I never thought I'd see you two boozing it up!" he boomed.

Grace fixed him with a baleful look. "I don't think one Margarita qualifies as 'boozing it up,' as you should well know."

Jack smirked. "All right. All right. Don't get your undies in a bunch. Let's just call it, 'making a good start.' I suppose it would be pushing it to ask you two if you'd like to smoke a little weed later."

Frances rounded on him. "Let's show a little respect here, mister." Turning to Alex, she sniffed, "This is what Grace was talking about, that some people aren't happy for her and might try to spoil her party."

Jack held up his hands in surrender. "Look, I'm pleased that Disney talked to Grace about her books. Really. And I don't mean to be throwing cold water on her party, but she should know that these deals don't usually work out. Lots of things can go wrong along the way. Am I right, Neil?"

Neil LeRoy puckered his lips. "Yeah, of course. I mean, any kind of deal can go south; not just a movie deal. But, I think attracting the attention of Disney Studios is cause for celebration. No one has talked to me about making any of my books into a movie." He raised his glass towards Grace. "I say, let's drink to your good fortune, and hope for the best!"

Alex relaxed her facial muscles, and took a sip out of her upraised glass. Looking at Matthew, she asked, "So, are all of you going to join us, or what?"

"Yeah, sure. Sorry we're late. Jack and I met up with Neil at the end of the show today. He wanted to look over the books of some of the new authors, and offer encouragement. Is this an extra chair?"

Alex tipped it back. "Sure. Have a seat.

"Neil seems like a really nice guy," she said, as he sat down. "Very down to earth, especially when you consider that he's such a celebrity."

"He is that. I guess he remembers what it was like to work hard writing a novel that didn't get noticed.

"I saw Marla Page hanging around, too, talking to some of the authors at the end of the day."

Alex looked up from her drink. "Oh, really? That's funny. She told me she left early to do some shopping. She probably saw some authors she knew," she added with a shrug.

Glancing at her watch she said, "We should get going to the square pretty soon. How are you doing, Grace? You're not discouraged by anything Jack said, are you?"

"Not at all. I told you I'm not going to let anyone spoil this time for me. I'm ready for whatever happens."

Wednesday morning

Chapter 16

ALEX AWOKE BEFORE her seven A.M. wake-up call. Sitting up in bed, she slowly stretched her arms and legs, turning her thoughts to the previous evening.

She felt that it had gone well enough, although she hadn't seen anyone talking to Grace about Disney's interest in her Benny books. In fact, Grace had been virtually ignored, so that she felt responsible to keep her company along with Frances. After Grace's one breakout Margarita at Sloppy Joe's, she had returned to sobriety, and seemed to lose her party spirit, in general.

By the time the group arrived at Mallory Square, the sunset celebration had been underway for over an hour. Mingling with the crowd, they had dispersed to watch the dozens of entertainers, including a juggling aerial artist, singers, magicians, clowns, flame swallowers, and even sidewalk preachers.

At precisely 6:05 p.m., the orange orb of a sun seemed to sink into the Gulf of Mexico, which drew enthusiastic applause and cheers from the throng of onlookers.

Afterwards, the crowd started breaking up, with many people making their way back into Old Town to continue partying at the bars and eateries.

Alex had rounded up her group to propose that they have dinner at a nearby rooftop restaurant she knew. There seemed to be unanimous agreement, until Jack said he'd go. Then, Grace and Frances said they were going to walk on the beach and eat at a crab shack, instead. That had been the end of Grace's party, at least with her being present.

The outdoor restaurant had been a big success for the others. Much of the conversation had centered on the seminar. Neil LeRoy had been peppered with questions about his successful career, and how he managed to get accepted by a major publisher.

Matthew had sat next to her, which incited Flossie, on her other side, to poke her whenever the man made a comment to her.

After an extended dinner, with drinks afterwards, the group separated. Some opted to continue the evening visiting more pubs on Duval, while others, including Alex, returned to the hotel.

She waited for a while in the lobby for Frances and Grace, but when they didn't turn up, she figured they had probably gotten back before she had, and had gone up to their room.

Right now, she had to get out of bed and start thinking about preparing for this day, starting with showering and dressing. Since there was a full schedule of lectures and panels, she decided she'd wear one of her better outfits. She would most likely be selling books at the tables, to help out the authors.

Just then, the phone rang, reminding her that she was supposed to be getting up. She lifted up the receiver and dropped it back down. *All right, already. I'm coming. I'm coming.*

***

A HALF HOUR LATER, she was stepping into the tiny elevator, followed in by two other women and three men, squishing her into a corner. Looking up, she again noticed the "MAXIMUM 6 PERSON OCCUPANCY" sign and chuckled to herself. Calculating the combined weight of the passengers that she could see from behind the wide body in front of her, she wondered, wouldn't a *pound* restriction be more relevant as to what the cables could safely withstand?

When the elevator stopped, she was relieved to see that they were on the main floor. After exiting, she walked by the doorway to the lobby and glanced in. Sitting on one of the sofas was the female impersonator, Fonda Dix, with another man who looked familiar. Studying his smooth face and expressive eyes, it came to her that he was the "Marilyn Monroe" impersonator who acted as emcee of the comedy show next door. Shaking her head in wonder at the remarkable transformation made with makeup, she turned down the hallway toward the dining room.

When she got there, she saw that it was crowded again, but she quickly spotted Grace, Frances, Flossie, and Cynthia at a table near the window. The O'Learys and Virgil were at another table nearby. As she walked over to join the women, she waved a greeting to the others and sat down between Flossie and Grace.

"Morning, ladies," she said brightly. To Grace and Frances she added, "I waited around for you last night when I got back to the hotel." They looked at her, suspiciously. "I just wanted to make sure that you were all right since you had gone off by yourselves. That's all."

Grace harrumphed, "You don't have to worry about us. We can take care of ourselves."

"O-kay then." Alex picked up a menu. "Well, I see they have French toast today. I'll have that."

"That's a good choice, dear," Flossie said. "We all need to have a full breakfast today. We might not be able to take a lunch break."

Their waitress, seeing Alex's upraised hand, came over and took her order.

After she left, Alex leaned on her elbows, looking at Flossie and inadvertently nudging Benny. "That's what I wanted to talk to you about. I'd really like to help out selling books today, so whoever wants to, can leave. I'm familiar with swiping credit cards. If someone could just take a couple minutes to show me how to keep track of the sales –"

Grace moved Benny out of her way. "You don't know our books to try to sell them. We might as well leave an 'honors box.'"

"Gee, thanks," Alex responded. "First of all, I've read a couple of them. But, don't you all write a synopsis on the backs that will induce someone to buy them?"

Cynthia took a book out of her purse. "Exactly. Here's my latest, *Dream Lover*. On the back it says, 'Christine thought she had met the perfect man. Devon Lowell was handsome, rich and attentive. And then suddenly he was gone, leaving no trace of himself – where he had lived, or where he had worked. Was he even real? It was as though she had imagined him.

"'When she discovers an unfamiliar key, she knows that if she can find what it unlocks, she'll have the answer to her question.'

108

"That should be enough to get someone's attention," Cynthia said with confidence.

"It certainly has mine," Alex replied, her eyebrows raised in surprise.

"Of course the backs and flyleaves are written to entice people to buy," Flossie agreed. "And I'll be happy to show you our simple method of recording sales for each author. It's not rocket science."

The waitress came back with Alex's breakfast and briskly set about refilling everyone's coffee, dripping a little on the table. Grace looked horrified as a drop landed near Benny. Grabbing up the puppet, she carefully placed him on her lap and put a protective arm over him.

Glancing sideways, Alex disregarded the little fuss, and greedily tucked into her food. "Mmmm, good."

Frances dabbed at her thin lips with her napkin, having just finished her scrambled eggs. "Well, I plan on spending most of the day at the table. Ms. Green from Disney might be stopping by, so I'm not leaving anything to chance."

"I guess that would be *me*." Alex made a little moue before taking another bite of syrupy French toast. "No, that's fine, Frances. I'm sure we can work well together."

Grace checked her watch and stared out the window, drumming her fingers on the table.

"Suit yourself," Frances said.

Grace stood up, scraping her chair. "Well, you people do what you want. I'm going up to the room before we need to leave for the seminar."

Alex held up her finger as she finished chewing. "Grace, just so you know, I saw Fonda Dix sitting in the lobby when I passed by. He was with the Marilyn Monroe impersonator, I think."

"Fonda Dix is in the lobby?" Grace looked stricken.

"He was, yes."

A siren could be heard in the distance.

Frances pushed back her chair and picked up her basket with Trixie inside. "I'll go with you, Grace. I'm done."

The wails continued getting louder and more piercing until they seemed to be coming from right below the window.

Alex jumped to her feet. "I think an emergency vehicle is here at the hotel. Let' go see what this is all about. We might need to evacuate, or something."

Flossie sighed deeply as she set down her coffee. "You'd think a person could just have a nice pleasant breakfast without all this upset all the time."

Cynthia grabbed her purse and slid off her chair. "We'd better go, Flossie."

Several other guests had gotten up and were walking out of the dining room, including Ethan, Joan, and Virgil. When they reached the doorway to the lobby, security personnel were blocking access.

Alex wormed her way through the bystanders to get up front. Speaking to the uniformed guard, she asked, "What's happened? Is there some emergency we need to know about?"

"No, Miss. Nothing to do with any of the other residents. Seems one of our guests was feeling poorly, so an ambulance was called. I'm sure he'll be revived and return to full health."

"Be revived? Did he have a heart attack? Look, I'm the tour director of a group staying here. I need to know if it was someone I'm responsible for."

The guard's brow furrowed as he considered her request. "Well, I guess it's not a secret. Although, you could probably find out if you called the hospital."

"I'm asking *you.*"

"Oh, all right. It makes sense you know if it's one of your people or not, but I can tell you it's not. It was Paul Robbins, a comedian from Miami. He's staying with us while he appears next door."

Alex's mouth dropped open. "Did you say he's a comedian from Miami? You don't mean Fonda Dix, do you?"

The guard's face flushed. "I do believe that's his stage name, yes, Miss."

Chapter 17

ALEX TURNED AROUND TO LOOK for Grace and Frances to tell them the news, but she didn't see them anywhere in the area. Grace would probably think that Fonda Dix's illness was poetic justice. Of course, no one wanted the man to die because he had made a few bad jokes, but the security guard had said that Fonda Dix, or Paul, was just "feeling poorly." Still, his needing to be "revived" sounded serious.

People were now streaming in from the dining room and coming down from the upper floors to see what all the commotion was about. It was human nature to be morbidly curious about the arrival of an ambulance. After all, emergencies were, by definition, exciting departures from the normal course of events.

Alex saw that the most helpful thing she could do would be to just get out of the way. The hotel probably wouldn't be forthcoming with any more information about Paul Robbins' condition, anyway.

She should go up to her room, freshen up, grab what she would need for the day, and report for duty as a salesclerk. Should be fun working all day with the ill-tempered Frances, with the creepy Trixie. At least Frances hadn't brought the doll along on the dinner cruise. Maybe she thought that it would be affected by the cool damp air.

Alex started over to the elevator, wondering if it might not be easier to just walk up three flights of stairs. Making her way through a cluster of people, she bumped into Virgil Meade.

As he pressed on the button to go up, he turned towards her, his eye sparkling with excitement. "Miss Trotter, did you hear about that female impersonator who was taken to the hospital? Must have OD'ed,"

"The security guard told me he had a heart attack, Virgil."

"A heart attack can be brought on by drugs. You know those entertainers. He was only in his thirties. It must have been something unnatural that caused it. It's so sad to be cut down in the prime of your life when you have so much more to live for. Puts me in mind of Robert Frost's lines,

'The woods are lovely, dark and deep,
But I have promises to keep.
And miles to go before I sleep
And miles to go before I sleep.'

"I know that poem!" Alex crowed.

Virgil's eyes glazed over. "*Everybody* knows that poem. It's taught in grade school." He jabbed at the button again.

She pressed her lips together. "Fine. Anyway, the man's name is Paul Robbins. And he's not *dying*, according to the security guard."

Virgil sighed. "Oh, I'm sure the security guard is quite the diagnostician."

"Look, Virgil, I saw Mr. Robbins sitting in the lounge when I was on my way to breakfast. He was fully conscious and talking to his friend Marilyn Monroe." She flapped her hand. "Oh, you know ... the actor who impersonates her. Here's the elevator."

The doors opened and three passengers exited. Alex and Virgil got on, just as Ethan came along to hold the door open. "Can Joan and I go up with you two?"

Alex chuckled. "Of course. It's supposedly safe for six people of any size."

The O'Learys stepped in, followed by three shapely young women wearing shorts and tank tops.

"Uh..." Alex started to object, as Ethan held up a hand to silence her.

"It's okay," he said quietly over her shoulder. "At least I'm not going to complain about attractive young women pressing against me."

Joan playfully poked him. "I've wondered why you never take the stairs."

***

TWO HOURS LATER Alex was satisfied that she was competently handling sales, filling out the receipts, and recording the transactions, just as she had been instructed by Flossie.

Unfortunately, after Flossie left for a seminar, Frances had assumed the role of "Trainer in Chief," who found fault with everything Alex was doing. According to Frances, the sales book should be kept "under the table," not out where Flossie had it. Also, she was criticized for either being "too friendly" with one customer, or "not talking enough" to another. She should be recording in a "blue pen," and not a black one.

When Alex straightened a pile of books next to Trixie, it seemed that even the doll was looking at her with disapproval.

***

AT NOON, ALEX WAS HEARTENED to see Grace walk up, thinking she might be coming to relieve her; but that didn't turn out to be the case. She had only stopped by to let Frances know that she would be meeting with Lorna Green later, and that she would show her one of Frances's books as she had promised.

After Grace left, Frances didn't seem to care about what ink Alex used, where she kept the sales book, or what she said to the customers. She had zoned out into a world of her own, staring off into space, thrumming her fingers on the table, ignoring the customers. After a while, she stood behind one of the chairs and mindlessly rocked it back and forth. This was followed by pacing behind the tables like a caged animal.

Not able to take it anymore, Alex grabbed her by the shoulders in midstride. "Frances, you're a nervous wreck! Why don't you take off for a while? Go get a cup of coffee, or something. Give me your cell number. If I see Grace, or Lorna Green anywhere nearby, I'll call you immediately. You're wound up like a top. You need to just relax."

Frances seemed to be paying attention, so she continued. "I should tell you that I overheard Ms. Green, yesterday, telling her assistant that she had several interviews set up for today, so I know that she's probably not just walking around.

"Anyway, both you and Grace have written good books that are loved by your readers, which is the most important reward for your efforts. And, if they're right for some project that Ms. Green has in mind, I'm sure she won't have any trouble contacting you. You need to calm down, and let your books stand on their own right now."

Frances looked thoughtful. "Maybe you're right. I should get away from here for a few minutes. I know I'm not helping matters by standing here working myself into a frenzy. I'll leave Trixie here to attract Ms. Green's attention if she does happen to come around.

"Be sure you call me if you see Ms. Green or Grace. I won't be long. Maybe I'll go outside, get some air, and have a little something to eat. I do feel light-headed."

Alex breathed a sigh of relief after Frances left, when two middle-aged women came over to the table.

"Are you ladies looking for any particular genre? There are many different ones here to choose from."

"We both love Romances," the lady in a lavender blouse and beige stretch pants answered with a giggle.

"Wonderful. We have three fine writers of romance. Take a look at this latest book by Cynthia Hart, for instance." She handed her a copy of *Dream Lover.*

"Is this a good one?"

"It's one I'd like to read," she answered truthfully. "Just look at the back and you'll see what I mean."

Five minutes later, she had completed the sale of three copies of the book, sending them off in paper bags bearing the OPAL's logo of an open book and a quill pen. As the women walked away, Alex gave herself a thumb's up under the table. Out of the corner of her eye, she thought she saw Trixie scowling at her.

***

BY THREE O'CLOCK, there still hadn't been any word from Grace or Lorna Green. Nevertheless, Frances had become focused and subdued, although her help wasn't needed then as there was very little traffic, or chores to do.

As Alex sat idly flipping through Cynthia's *Dream Lover*, Flossie came rushing over, her face flushed. "Alex! I'm glad you're still here," she gasped. "I wanted to be the one to tell you." She paused again to catch her breath.

"What's wrong, Flossie? Did something happen to someone in our group?"

Flossie shook her head and waved her hand until she could speak again. "No, nothing to do with us. It's that Fonda Dix character. He's … dead!"

Alex stared, wide-eyed. "Oh, no! I thought he was going to be okay. How did he die?"

"It was a heart attack. Like they said. I guess it was a really bad one that they couldn't save him."

Frances had come over from the other table. "Grace will be happy to hear this."

Alex turned towards her. "Happy?"

Frances distractedly brushed off the front of her blouse. "Forget I said that. I should have said that she won't be *un*happy."

Alex nodded. "I know what you mean, but it's a still a shame considering that he was so young. Only in his thirties." She stared off into space, and said under her breath, "I wonder if he *was* on drugs."

117

Wednesday afternoon

Chapter 18

WITH A HALF HOUR LEFT in the day, most of the authors had started straightening up their areas; not that there was much to do, since all the books would be left in place. The writers were just bored due to the lack of business, and anxious to get back to their hotels to start their evenings.

Frances told Alex that she could go early, since she hadn't been "trained" on how to reconcile the sales report with the contents of the cash box. Since Alex wanted to leave, anyway, she didn't point out that she regularly kept track of thousands of dollars in tour payments. It had been a long and trying day with Frances, who had vacillated between having high anxiety and deep depression. The woman had been a nightmare.

But, Alex thanked her for closing up, and went on her way, deciding to walk around some before she left the building. In the first room she entered, she noticed that many authors had left their tables to visit with one another, probably comparing sales and discussing how the event was going.

It didn't seem like a good time for her to stop and look at the books, as she would be interrupting the authors and bringing them back to their tables.

As she was about to leave, she noticed Marla Page standing by one of the vacated tables. To Alex, it looked like she was up to something, the way her eyes darted around the room. As she watched in disbelief, Marla picked up a couple of books, slipped them into her valise, and moved on to another vacated table.

Why was Marla Page stealing books? Whatever the reason, she needed to intervene, and in a hurry. Calling over to Marla, the woman looked up, startled at first, before scowling as Alex crossed over to her.

"Hi, Marla. Find any good books?"

"I'm sure some are okay," she answered brusquely, then looked at her watch. "Uh, it's about closing time. You're going to have to leave."

"Yeah, I will. I was just going to tell you that the author of these books is right over there. The woman in the red sweater. I figured you wanted to know who to pay."

Marla looked daggers at her. "Right. I was about to do that before you stopped me."

"I'm sure you were. I was just trying to be helpful. I'll see you later. Everyone's doing their own thing for dinner. It's been a long day."

***

Alex was dragging by the time she walked the six blocks back to the C'est La Vie. Trudging up the hotel steps, she decided that what she needed was a nice chilled glass of chardonnay. She'd stop at the bar before she went up to her room. Hopefully, someone from the group would be there for a little conversation, too.

Quickening her pace, she started across the lobby, curious as to why so many people were standing around talking. Oh, yeah. They must be discussing the untimely death of Fonda Dix.

Looking around, she didn't see anyone she knew, so she turned down the hallway to the barroom. Pushing open the glass door, she felt comforted by the cool, dimly lit space, as "Misty" was being played by the pianist. Several couples were seated and talking quietly; some at tables, while others sat on bar stools.

Glancing down the bar to find a place, she was surprised to see the man she had identified as Marilyn Monroe sitting on the end stool. Making her way over, she slipped onto the stool next to his.

After the bartender took her order, she glanced at "Marilyn" out of the corner of her eye. He was cradling his drink, and staring straight ahead, oblivious to her.

The bartender delivered her glass of wine that she quickly picked up and sipped from, gratefully.

Casually rearranging herself on the stool, she managed to make eye contact with the man and smiled. "Pardon me, but aren't you the Marilyn Monroe impersonator?" He barely nodded in answer. "You do a fabulous imitation of her."

"Thanks," he mumbled.

"I believe that you were a friend of uh, Paul Robbins, who played Fonda Dix. I heard that he passed away today, and I just wanted to tell you how sorry I am. It must have been a shock for you. For everyone. He was still so young."

"He was thirty-two. *Thirty-two.*" His mouth twisted in bitterness. "We were *more* than friends. We'd been together for years, playing the circuit."

"Oh, I see." She drew in a breath and let it out slowly. "Um, my name is Alex Trotter, by the way. I'm a tour director staying here with my group of authors who are here for the Literary Seminar."

He focused his troubled grey eyes on her for the first time. "I'm John Austin. Nice to meet you."

"I saw Paul's act. He was a real crowd-pleaser."

"Yeah. He was funny. He could be pretty outrageous, but he was a good man. I just can't believe he's gone." He looked down, pressing a balled fist against his mouth.

Alex nodded, sympathetically. "I can imagine. Had he been sick? I mean, I know he was sick, but, you know ... for a while?"

"No, that's just the thing. I thought he was fine when we came down for breakfast, when he suddenly complained about a sharp pain in his chest. I got him over to a sofa in the lobby where he seemed to weaken, until he actually slumped down. I ran to the desk for help, and they called for an ambulance."

"How awful! Had he ever been diagnosed with a heart condition?"

"No. Not that I know of, and I think he would have told me. And he never mentioned heart trouble being in his family, either."

John drained his drink and signaled for another. When it was set down in front of him, she asked, "Would you say that Paul took good care of himself?"

He turned to look at her. "That's another thing. He was one of the healthiest people I ever knew. Kept himself in shape, ate sensibly, didn't drink to excess, didn't smoke ..."

Alex saw her opening. "So, he didn't use drugs?"

"I never knew him to take anything stronger than an aspirin. And I would have known. He was almost paranoid about ingesting any kind of 'foreign substance' that could have a side effect."

Alex's forehead scrunched up in confusion. "What did the doctor say was the cause of death?"

John shrugged, helplessly. "Heart attack. That's all I know. There were no other symptoms."

Alex tugged at her hair. "Aren't they going to do an autopsy? I mean, healthy thirty-two olds don't just drop dead from heart attacks."

"I asked about that. From what I was told, they don't do an autopsy unless there's a question about the cause of death, or they suspect foul play. Besides, only a family member can request one. Paul and I have only lived together in Florida, so our relationship couldn't be recognized as a legal union. That leaves me without any rights as a survivor." He shook his head and scowled.

"Paul has a sister in New York who'll be coming down tomorrow to plan a memorial service, or whatever, so maybe she could ask."

Alex patted his arm. "I think that would help you to be able to accept his passing. His friends in the club must be in shock, too. Are they cancelling the show for tonight?"

"No, we can't do that. You know the theater – the 'show must go on' and all that. They'll probably do a thirty-second blackout as a memorial."

His eyes lit up remembering something. "Paul had a new act he was going to be trying out tonight."

"Oh, yeah? What was that?" Alex asked, idly pleating her napkin.

"Well, he had had some fun with a customer who had brought a beaver puppet to the show. So Paul got one and wrote some jokes, for it, using it as a prop. You know what I mean by 'beaver jokes.'"

Alex wasn't able to speak as she could only gape at him, dumbfounded.

Wednesday evening

Chapter 19

THAT EVENING, ALEX SAT on her bed absently tracing the pattern of her floral bedspread with her finger, while her mind went back over the conversation she had had with John Austin. Considering all that he had told her about Fonda Dix, it seemed impossible that he had died from natural causes. And then, when John had off-handedly mentioned that Fonda got a beaver puppet for his act, everything pointed to Grace Tuttle as being his murderer. But could Grace actually kill the man for embarrassing her? That was hard to believe. She'd have to be a monster to take someone's life as punishment for making bad jokes at her expense. Or, could someone else have taken revenge on behalf of Grace? That was even more ludicrous. Frances was the only one who even liked her.

And, what was her own responsibility knowing what she knew? She couldn't just sit by and let somebody get away with murder; and yet, she couldn't be sure that Fonda Dix had actually been murdered, much less that Grace was his killer. The only way that the cause of death could be determined was to have an autopsy done. But, John had said that he had no legal standing to request one, and the doctor hadn't found the cause of death suspicious to order one.

She picked up the phone and dialed a familiar number. It was answered after only two rings.

"Hey, Arlie. It's me. Alex."

"Well, finally. I've been waiting to hear from you. Nothing's wrong, is there? I mean, no one's been murdered or anything?" His voice was light with teasing.

"Arlie, what a thing to say. Well, okay, you might be right, but I'm not sure."

"You're not sure if a person's been murdered? As a homicide detective, maybe I can help you out. If a dead guy's got a bullet hole in his head, or a knife in his back, he's probably been murdered."

She rolled her eyes. "Thanks. I'm serious, Arlie. A female impersonator from the club next door died today of a heart attack. But he was only thirty-two years old. I think he might have been murdered."

"Alex, not everyone lives to be 80. And they don't call a medical examiner to investigate a death just because somebody is only thirty-two. Did a doctor find it to be a suspicious death?"

"No. But I did."

"Oh … well, then."

"Listen, Arlie, there's more to it. This Fonda Dix guy taunted one of my authors during his act. She was mortified, and I'm afraid that she may have killed him."

"His stage name is Fonda Dix? Hah! Maybe he died laughing. How do you think your author lady killed him?"

"I'm guessing she poisoned him. Yesterday, I went to a seminar given by a former forensic toxicologist. She talked about some of the poisons that have been used to murder people. Apparently, they break down quickly in the body, so they aren't easily detected after death."

He chuckled softly. "So you studied lethal toxins for a *whole hour* before you could determine the cause of death of someone you didn't know."

"All right, smart ass. What I *learned* is that even small amounts of certain poisons can kill a person. Oh, one thing I forgot to tell you is that Grace, the suspect, is a nurse, so she would know what poisons to use and how to use them."

Arlie's voice turned serious. "Alex, just because this nurse knows about lethal toxins, doesn't mean she has *access* to them, or to *him,* more to the point. What drugs are you talking about, for instance?"

"Just a minute, let me look at my notes." She dug in her purse and pulled out her notebook. "Okay, the most popular 'murder drug,' if you can call it that, is Ethylene-glycol. That's what's in anti-freeze that you can get at the nearest gas station. It's colorless, odorless, and has a sweet taste that can be disguised in something like lemonade."

"You said the guy died of a heart attack."

"That's right. Why?"

"Well, ethylene-glycol causes diarrhea, vomiting, and disorientation at first, and then vital organs start to fail, starting with the kidneys, and finally, the heart stops. The doctor wouldn't have said the patient just died from a heart attack.

"What other poison do you think could have been used?"

Alex scanned her notes. "I'm glad to hear you're taking this seriously. The next one I have listed here is Suc-cin-yl-choline, however you say it. That breaks down quickly, so it can't be detected. I don't know where you get it."

Arlie chuckled. "'SUX,' as its called, is a paralytic used in hospitals for procedures like inserting trach tubes, and in prisons, as part of a three-part cocktail to execute people. It would be impossible for a nurse to legally obtain it. It's locked up and inventoried wherever it's used − to prevent it from being taken home to kill somebody, for example.

"And, again, it wouldn't cause a heart attack. A person would become totally paralyzed, but stay conscious for hours until he died of suffocation when the muscles around his lungs could no longer move. What else have you got?"

"Okay, the last one I wrote down is potassium chloride − and that stops the heart! Also, it can't be detected after death because it's salt, and salt is natural to the body. And it can be purchased in a grocery store. How about that?"

Arlie rubbed his eyes. "Okay, that's a possibility, although a medical examiner could detect it if he's looking for it. Actually, potassium chloride is the third part of the 'execution cocktail.' It's also one of the drugs 'recommended' on those suicide internet sites, which is pretty gruesome. Two problems using it to murder someone: it's hard to know how much for a fatal dosage and, if injected, it's very painful and the site becomes red and swollen. That would have been noticed by the doctor, not to mention the patient. You'd need to take a lot orally, but it would more likely cause arrhythmia than a heart attack."

Alex sighed in exasperation. "Well, that's all I've got. There are probably others, but that's all that I learned in *one hour*," she snickered.

Arlie shrugged. "Hey, that's pretty good for one hour. More to the point is – motive. Why would somebody murder a stranger over an insult, unless they're mentally unbalanced. Is she?"

Alex pursed her lips. "No, I wouldn't say that. Grace is a little odd, though. She's the one I told you about who wears a beaver hand puppet all the time."

"Oh, her. Well, she's probably used to being teased. That wouldn't be much of a motive for her."

"This is serious, Arlie. What you don't seem to realize is that Fonda Dix deeply offended her in every way you can imagine, and then he went and got a beaver puppet to put into his comedy routine. She may have found out about that, although I don't know that for a fact."

"If you didn't know before, how could she have known? Babe, I know that you're concerned, but there's just no probable cause to investigate Grace, or anyone else, from what you've told me."

Alex screwed up her mouth into a pout. "I know. That's why there has to be an autopsy done. Fonda's partner John wants one to help him come to terms with his death, and I'd like to see if there's any merit in my suspicion, or to clear Grace in my own mind. John can't request one because he's not family. There's a sister coming down from New York to make funeral arrangements, but he doesn't know if she'll want one done. You know how squeamish people get thinking about a loved one's body being disfigured in that way, right?"

He nodded. "True. But in any jurisdiction I know of, a close friend can order an independent autopsy. I'd think that would be the case in Florida."

Her face lit up. "Oh, good. I'll tell John. If he can't, do you think you could order one from the coroner?"

127

"No, no. Don't even go there. For you, I'll look into the matter when I get there and, if it looks suspicious to me, I'll *talk* to the ME.

"Don't get any more involved with this, Alex. If it is murder, the killer probably isn't some middle-aged writer of childrens books. You could end up as the guy's next target."

She looked at the ceiling thinking how to answer him. "You're right. It probably isn't Grace. Anyway, don't worry about me. I won't investigate anything that isn't any of my business."

He shook his head in defeat. "Fine. And I'll pretend that you didn't just make a promise that is so open to interpretation, it's totally meaningless."

She smiled to herself in acknowledgment.

His voice softened. "I'll say good night, babe. Call me if you have any problem, whatsoever."

"*That's* a promise, Arlie."

Thursday morning

Chapter 20

ALEX SCANNED THE DINING ROOM the next morning, looking for John Austin. Not seeing him, she noticed that Flossie was waving her over to join her, Grace and Frances.

Alex started to make her way over, thinking that this would be a good opportunity to gauge Grace's reaction to the death of Fonda Dix; but she had to bring it up in such a way that she didn't reveal her suspicions.

When she got to the table, she sat next to Flossie and across from Grace and Frances. Oddly enough, there was no sign of Benny. "Morning. Nice to see everyone. But where's Benny, Grace?"

"What? Why do you ask?"

"Why do I ask? Because he's *always* with you, that's why. He was with you at breakfast yesterday, for instance."

"I don't think so." Grace twisted her mouth in displeasure, pulling the collar of her blouse up under her chin. Looking around anxiously she called out, "Where's that waitress?! I need more coffee!"

Alex stared at her. "That's one reason that I know Benny was here yesterday. Don't you remember, when the waitress brought more coffee, she carelessly spilled some, and you took Benny off the table to prevent him from getting coffee on him."

Grace set her jaw. "I don't think that was yesterday. It must have been the day before. What difference does it make? Anyway, Benny's up in our room. There aren't any children staying here, so I don't need to bring him down all the time. I'll get him after breakfast to take him to the seminar."

Becoming more suspicious of Grace since she lied about Benny not having been there the day before, Alex pushed ahead to keep her talking. "Oh, speaking of the seminar, how did your meeting go with Lorna Green yesterday? Did she like Frances's Trixie stories?"

Grace curled her upper lip, exposing her two front teeth. "She didn't say much about them. I don't think they were what she was looking for. I tried my best." She glanced sideways at Frances who was glaring back at her.

"I thought you said −" Frances started, her face flushed.

"I said she *might* be interested. Who knows? I'm not a psychic. And I'm certainly not your agent, Frances. I see that no good deed goes unpunished."

Alex smelled blood in the water. "Well then, how about your Benny stories. Is Ms. Green still interested in them?"

Grace jerked her head up. "Of course she is. She even took a picture of Benny to send to Hollywood. Other than that, she was too busy to get into much conversation. She said that she'd get back to me today."

She glanced at Frances. "Maybe she'll contact you today, too."

Flossie broke in. "Well, that sounds very promising. Here's our waitress. Let's order, shall we?"

After the waitress departed, Alex tried another gambit with Grace. "I'll be crossing my fingers for both of you. It's still the best news we've had here at the seminar. Speaking of news," she continued, trying not to wince at the awkward segue, "did you two hear about that comedian Fonda Dix dying yesterday?"

Grace stared down at her placemat. "He was no comedian, but, yeah, we heard."

"It's all that everybody in the hotel is talking about," Frances added.

Grace raised her head and fixed her beady eyes on Alex. "He died of a heart attack. I can't say I'm upset about it. Should I be? He was a vulgar, perverse man who mocked decent people to make cheap jokes. He didn't care about my feelings, so why should I care that he's dead?"

The waitress stopped at their table with a coffee pot, and Alex nodded that she wanted a warm-up. "I didn't say you should *care,* Grace. I know you had every reason to dislike him. I only thought his death was unfortunate, and even shocking, because he was only thirty-two years old. Way too young to die of a heart attack, don't you think?"

Grace looked uncomfortable, fidgeting with her napkin and moving around in her seat. "I'm sure there are many cases of people dying at that age. Can't we talk about something else?"

"Yes, that's a good idea, Grace," Flossie put in, moving her silverware to make space for the waitress to put down her soft-boiled egg and an English muffin.

Alex leaned forward, smiling. "Well, I do have something to tell you that I think you'll like hearing.

131

I've made reservations for us all to go on a dinner cruise tonight on a catamaran boat."

Flossie clapped her hands. "Oh, what fun! I was hoping to get out on the water! What time and everything?"

"We should meet no later than five-fifteen at the dock on William Street. Sailing's at five-thirty. The cruise will last for two hours, so we'll see the sunset out on the water, of course.

"Dinner will be buffet-style with Caribbean food, like roast pork in mojo, grilled chicken marinated in pineapple juice, and deep fried plantains. There'll be two free bars, one on each deck. After dinner, there'll be live reggae music for dancing. It does sound like fun, doesn't it?"

Frances's shoulders drooped. "Oh, great – free bars. That means I have to put up with more drunks than usual."

Grace didn't comment as she kept her head down eating her blueberry pancakes.

Alex directed her attention to Flossie and Frances. "Well, good. I'm glad it appeals to you. I thought it would be a nice break from selling books and attending lectures.

"It will be so romantic to dance onboard a ship out on the Gulf of Mexico at sunset," Flossie enthused. "I only hope there will be some men to dance with."

Alex chuckled. "First, it's just a *boat*, Flossie, not a ship. And there should be enough men. The capacity is something like 50, so I would expect to see a lot of other people there from the seminar. I can't promise, but there might well be some unattached men here for the seminar who will be on the cruise."

"We don't need men to eat dinner on a boat," Grace grumbled.

Alex sighed. Looking around, she spotted the others from the group at various other tables. "Uh, would you ladies excuse me? I see more of our group here, and I need to catch up with them to tell them about tonight before they leave."

"Certainly, dear," Flossie answered sweetly. "That reminds me. We have Jack and Matthew to dance with." She winked at Alex.

Alex got to her feet. "And Virgil. Don't forget about Virgil." She grinned at Flossie before she headed over to Ethan and Joan O'Leary's table.

***

AFTER HAVING GONE AROUND the room to tell the others about the dinner cruise, she was about to leave when she spotted John Austin sitting alone at a small table reading the newspaper.

Unsure that he would even remember her, or welcome her company, she cautiously approached. "John?"

"Alex! Hi!" He smiled as he put down his paper and pulled back a chair. "Have a seat."

"Thanks. I will. For just a minute, anyway. I won't intrude on your privacy for long, but I have something important to tell you so that you can get answers to your questions about Paul's death."

John's eyebrows rose in surprise. "You sure know how to make an entrance, I'll say that for you. Well, don't keep me in suspense. Talk. I'm all ears."

Chapter 21

ALEX LEFT THE DINING ROOM reassured that John Austin would arrange for an independent autopsy to be performed on his late partner's body. As he told her, Paul Robbins's sister was equally puzzled by the cause of death. Since she wouldn't be able to come down to Key West until the weekend, John felt confident that she would agree to let him handle it.

Up in her room, Alex looked around to see what she wanted to take with her for the day. Her plan was to first attend the morning seminar titled, "You Do Judge a Book by Its Cover." Afterwards, she'd check with her people to see it they needed help at their space before she walked around to look over the other authors' tables. She figured there were many good writers at the seminar she had never heard of. It would be fun to search them out, and maybe discover a few exciting new talents.

Her eyes fell on Marla Page's novel, *Screaming Bloody Murder,* which was the one book she hadn't read of the ones she had gotten from the OPAL group. On its cover was the Edvard Munch painting of "The Scream." It was an image of a person running into the foreground with hands clamped over the ears with the mouth open in a misshapen long "O."

Picking it up, she turned it over to read the back cover.

"For 19-year-old Caitlin Lee, Homecoming weekend promised to be a fun flurry of parties before and after the big game, culminating in a dance at her Kappa Beta Tau sorority house.

When alumnus Trevor Hill shows up and flirts with her, Caitlin can't believe her good fortune; that is, until he lures her into a back room where he brutally forces himself on her. Although overpowered and terrified, Caitlin finds her voice to scream for help.

Will anyone hear her and come to her rescue? Or will her screams bring about an even more horrific situation.

Be careful what you wish for."

Putting down the book, she gave it a couple pats. *Have to admit, it's got my interest. I'll start it when I get back this afternoon.*

Taking one more look around, she decided to take along a sweater, slung her purse over her shoulder, and made for the door.

***

WALKING INTO THE AUDITORIUM before the start of the lecture she noticed Matthew, who was already seated, motioning to her to join him.

"I should have known that *you'd* be here," she said with a smile as she slipped into the seat next to him. "I just wish that all these authors could see your graphic designs."

"You and me both. Here, let me help you with your sweater. It's chilly in here.

"Anyway, I have good news about getting work. Neil LeRoy wants me to do his next cover, and he's recommending me to some other big-name authors who said they'll contact me. Who knows? This could turn into a big deal for me. Now I'm torn if I should concentrate on promoting my art or my writing."

"Yeah, must be tough," Alex mocked. "Seriously, I thought your book *Gone* was a really good thriller. I've liked all the books I've read by your group. I'm going to start on Marla's latest this afternoon, if I have a chance. I want to look around at the books by the writers here who aren't well known. I bet there's some undiscovered talent here."

Matthew nodded. "I'm sure there is. You have to be more than a good writer to get recognition, and by 'recognition' I mean 'sales.' It takes a lot of hard work networking on social media, making the right connections; and getting a few lucky breaks along the way won't hurt either."

He gave her a playful nudge. "Get cards from the people who need better book covers."

***

AFTER THE LECTURE they made their way over to the OPAL exhibit. Alex was relieved to see that most of

136

the authors were there to take care of business, so that she wouldn't be needed to help out.

"Where's Grace?" she asked Flossie, looking around.

"Lorna Green's assistant Regina stopped by to tell her, and I quote, 'Miss Green requires your presence immediately,' unquote. You'd think she had an audience with the queen."

Alex looked impressed. "Oh, wow. I wonder what that means. Maybe she's going to ask Grace to sign a contract. Actually, I don't think she should do that without consulting an attorney, do you?"

"No, but I'm not sure you can negotiate with Lorna Green. She'd probably say, 'take it or leave it.' And she wouldn't care which."

Flossie waved her hand, dismissively. "Anyway, that was an hour ago, and we haven't heard from Grace since. Frances has been nervous as a cat on a porch full of rocking chairs. I'm not sure if she's nervous for Grace, or anxious about her own chances for stardom."

Alex grinned, cynically. "Her own. When I worked with Frances yesterday, she was a bundle of nerves after Grace took her book to Ms. Green. Then she settled down to doom and gloom. Well, Maybe Grace will have good news for us when we meet for the dinner cruise. For Frances, too, hopefully."

Flossie nodded. "Yes, that would be nice. Speaking of the romantic cruise tonight, I noticed you and Matthew were just together."

Alex rolled her eyes. "I said the cruise was for 'dinner,' and you said the cruise was for 'romance.' Anyway, you'll be disappointed to hear that we came here from a lecture on the importance of book covers."

Flossie patted her hand. "Oh, that's okay. I'm sure you'll have your chance." Alex sighed, audibly, shaking her head.

"I'll see you later, Flossie. I'm going to look for some good books by some of these authors I'm not familiar with."

***

ALEX SPENT THE NEXT couple of hours circulating around the hall talking to authors and perusing the backs of their books, deciding to purchase three promising mysteries.

Ready to return to the hotel, but taking one last look around, she was enticed to go over to see one more writer who had set up colorful posters of her book covers. The author was a dramatic-looking middle-aged woman whose dark hair had a white streak that swept across her forehead. Her name plate read, "Vera Blaze."

After a few minutes of conversation, Alex learned that 'Vera Blaze' was not a nom de plume, that she lived in Chicago, and that she was a self-published author of suspenseful mysteries.

Flipping through her books, Alex stopped dead at one of them titled, *Screams in the Night.* The cover was the same Edvard Munch painting of "The Scream" that was on Marla Page's book.

"Did you need to get permission to use that painting for your cover?" she asked.

"No," Vera replied, simply. "It's in the public domain because it was printed prior to 1923. I used it because it's the most recognizable image of a scream, so it's perfect for the title. I published this myself about three years ago."

Alex continued to puzzle over the cover, wondering at the coincidence of Marla using the same painting for her book with a similar title, although Alex had just learned in the lecture that covers using stock pictures and free-market artwork were non-exclusive.

"I've got more recent books," Vera offered, thinking Alex was not sold on that one.

"No, I'm interested in this one. What's it about?"

"It's about the rape of a college girl; but there's a twist. Take a look at the synopsis on the back cover."

Alex flipped it over and skimmed through it, her eyes widening as she read.

> *"Nineteen-year-old Callie Wilson was looking forward to Spring Fling weekend with its many parties, including the dance at her own sorority, Kappa Phi Omega.*
>
> *When heartthrob Jason Gregory arrives and showers her with attention, she is overjoyed until he tricks her into going into a back room where he forces her down on a sofa and sexually assaults her. Terrified, she summons the will to scream for help.*
>
> *But, will anyone hear her and come to her rescue? Or will her screams result in an even worse outcome.*
>
> ***Be careful what you wish for.***"

Alex looked up, ashen faced. "I'll take this one."

Thursday afternoon

Chapter 22

ENTERING THE LOBBY of the C'est La Vie, Alex was pleased to see John Austin, who was at the desk getting his mail. Waiting nearby, she called out to him as he started walking away sorting through his envelopes.

Hearing his name, he looked around. Seeing Alex, he smiled in recognition. "Oh, Alex. Just the person I want to see."

"Good. I was waiting here to ask you if there's been any news."

"Well, there's nothing conclusive, but I did want to tell you what's been happening. To be honest, I couldn't remember your last name. Why don't we sit over there." John indicated a pair of chairs in a back corner.

As they sat down Alex said, "Trotter."

"What?"

"Sorry. My last name is Trotter."

"Oh, that's right. I'll remember that. Anyway, after you told me this morning that I could arrange for an autopsy, I called Paul's sister Naomi, and she agreed that I should go ahead. But, when I was put in touch with a pathologist, I was told it would cost $5,000. That's a little steep for me right now; and for Naomi, when I told her.

"Anyway, I went back to the hospital and managed to talk to the doctor who had signed the death certificate. Turns out, he was also uneasy about his own finding. As I told him more about Paul, I guess he thought it even more unlikely, so he asked the hospital pathologist to take another look at the body. Guess what? The pathologist found a couple of needle marks."

"I knew it!" Alex exclaimed, on the edge of her seat.

He held up his hand. "Hold on. I'm sure that Paul didn't shoot up."

She emphatically shook her head. "No, no, I don't think so either. Like I told you this morning, I've been thinking that he was poisoned, and an injection could have been the means."

John's forehead was scrunched in confusion. I don't see how, without Paul's knowledge. Anyway, the doctor contacted the police to have the Medical Examiner do an autopsy. I asked if the ME could test for potassium chloride, like you suggested. I don't know if he will since I couldn't give him a good reason for that. I'm sure they're thinking heroin, or whatever."

Alex sat back on her hands. "Yeah, I can imagine. But the important thing is that they're doing an autopsy. You know they won't find narcotics, but they'll no doubt discover what it was that actually killed Paul. You did a good thing to honor your friend, John."

141

"Oh, I don't know. I just want answers to make some sense of this. Paul didn't have any enemies who would poison him, as you seem to think."

Alex didn't want to debate the point right then, so shrugged it off. "I just attended a seminar on poisons used in murder mysteries. Maybe I'm being influenced by that."

Thinking that it was a good time to change the subject, she asked, "So, how did it go at 'Some Like It Hot' last night?"

His shoulders sagged. "It was okay, I guess. We all supported each other to get through the show. Tonight we're dark as usual for Thursday."

She raised an eyebrow. "Oh, you mean you're closed." She let that sink in for a moment, then had an idea. "Hey, why don't you join my group for our dinner cruise tonight? I think it'd be good for you. There'll be a buffet supper, free bars, and live music for dancing. "

He jutted out his lower lip, considering. "Hmm. What time?"

"We're meeting at five-fifteen at the William Street dock. Whaddya think?"

He nodded, his face brightening. "I think I will. Thanks. You're right. I could use some distraction."

"Good. There are some interesting people in our group you'll like to talk to. Oh, wait a minute." She clamped her teeth over her bottom lip. "There's one thing I need to tell you. Remember that customer with the beaver puppet that Paul had fun with the other night?"

"Yeah. What about it?"

"That woman is Grace Tuttle. She's one of the authors in our group, and Benny the Beaver is a character in the books she writes for children. I think you better not say anything to her about Paul – or, as she knew him, Fonda Dix."

142

"I don't know that I would, but why not?"

"She was extremely upset by that incident. To be honest with you, I've even thought that she could have poisoned him."

"What?! Because he teased her? You've got quite an imagination, Alex."

"I know it does sound a little crazy, even to me when I say it out loud, but she's a pretty unstable woman. On the other hand, I don't have any proof. But when you told me that Paul was putting the beaver in his act, I thought that that could have unhinged her. Who all knew about that?"

"I don't know if *any*one else knew, but me. He changed his routine all the time, and liked to surprise the rest of us with new jokes.

"Anyway, now that you tell me about this Grace person, I think I should make a point of telling her that Paul was my partner. See what her reaction is. She might confess on the spot."

Alex gave him a look of mock resignation. "Okay, okay. Actually, that's a good idea. She probably won't react at all, and I can get this notion out of my head. Grace should be in good spirits tonight since she met with a Disney rep today who might have offered to option her book."

He sat up straight. "No kidding?"

"Well, it's not a sure thing, but maybe. Anyway, I have to get upstairs to check into something. We'll see you at the pier at five-fifteen, right?"

"Yeah, sure. Should be fun."

***

CROSSING THE LOBBY moments later, she was startled to see Grace disappear through the doorway into the elevator hallway. Anxious to hear about the

Disney contract, she quickened her pace and called out, "Grace! Grace!"

Grace turned to see who it was. Glowering at Alex, she scuttled off toward the elevator.

Alex gave up the pursuit, thinking, *Hmmm. I don't think it went so well with Disney.*

Thursday evening

Chapter 23

ALEX HAD TO WAIT for the elevator to come back down after Grace had commandeered it, not that she had wanted to share it with the bad-tempered woman, anyway. It was obvious from Grace's glare that she didn't want any company.

Given that she appeared to be in such a foul mood after her meeting with Lorna Green, it was a good guess that something had gone wrong with her budding deal with Disney. Alex knew better than to try to ask her about it. Eventually, it would probably come out. When it did, she hoped that people would be kind and offer some support. Grace would likely tell Frances what had happened, and Frances would be sympathetic although she was hoping for her own deal.

Upstairs in her room a few minutes later, Alex picked up her copy of Marla Page's novel and flopped down on the window seat with her canvas bag of books. Pulling out Vera Blaze's *Screams in the Night,* she put it side by side with S*creaming Bloody Murder,* and looked in amazement at the similarities. The covers, the titles, the synopses on the back covers, were almost identical. Checking the publication dates, she confirmed that Vera Blaze's book had been published three years before Marla's. At a glance, it was apparent that Marla had stolen the exact plot, characters, and design of Vera's book.

To investigate any further, she was going to have to read both of them to see how similar the interiors were. She decided to read chapter one of Vera's book, first, and then chapter one of Marla's, and so on, through to the ends of each book. She noted that both books had twenty-six chapters, but Marla's book was six pages longer.

Reading through chapter one of both books she was introduced to the protagonists, Callie, in Vera's, and Caitlin, in Marla's, with descriptions of her life in college, her friends, and her life in the sorority. Except for insignificant differences in details and in writing style, the two chapters were identical.

Seeing how similar they were, Alex felt that she would be able to read them side by side, rather than one at a time. Skimming through the next several chapters, it became more a game of "Spot the Differences" than of reading.

The twist in the story was the same in both books: at the point where Trevor/Jason is forcing himself on Callie/Caitlin at the party, she screams, which brings several sorority sisters to come to her rescue. After the young man has been subdued, the women continue to batter him with their high heels until even Callie/Caitlin pleads for them to stop. When they do, the dazed and bloodied young man attempts to flee, but is easily stopped and knocked down to the floor, where they tie his wrists and ankles with lamp cords.

He remains their captive for the next week, sitting on the sofa wearing restraints and a "RAPIST" sign around his neck. Since he graduated the year before, no one on their campus is looking for him.

While his physical wounds heal, the women subject him to various forms of mental and psychological torture. Hour after hour they play recordings of "It's a Small World," "The Yellow Submarine," and "Call Me, Maybe" on a loop until he screams for them to be turned off.

During the day, they turn on the TV to reruns of *The Golden Girls*, and *The Fresh Prince of Bel Air,* played over and over. At night, they repeatedly play the movies, *Heaven's Gate*, *Revenge of the Nerds*, and *Cat Woman*.

For meals, his hands are untied and he is brought into the dining room where he is placed in the corner wearing his "RAPIST" sign. The sorority women continue to enjoy themselves, talking and laughing, even as they ignore his very presence.

At the end of the week, several women come into his room, untie him and tell him he is free to go. But before he leaves, they caution him not to tell anyone about his captivity, to which he eagerly agrees.

At the door, he is sent off with a final caveat: If he breathes one word about his treatment, they will find out and have him arrested for a rape that was witnessed by *five women*. If convicted in a trial, he won't see the outside of a prison until he's at least middle-aged. "Have a good life."

Alex sat there, stunned. While the story was disturbing in both its subject and tone, she was incredulous that Marla Page had totally ripped off someone else's book, almost word for word. Checking Vera Blaze's book, she saw on the back side of the title page the familiar, "no part of this book may be

147

reproduced, scanned," etc. etc. "without permission of the author." How much is a "part?" If what Marla did was illegal, what was the penalty?

Obviously it would take a copyright attorney to render a legal opinion on what Marla had done, and it wasn't her place to pursue the issue. However, she had to do something about her discovery; she would make it known to the wrongdoer, and the person wronged.

Having decided that, a few minutes later she was standing outside Marla Page's room, knocking on her door.

"Who is it?" Marla asked from inside.

"It's Alex Trotter."

"What do you want?" Marla asked impatiently as she swung open the door. Her eyes fell down to Alex's hands. "What the hell?"

Alex was holding out the two books. "Do you want to explain this?"

"No. This doesn't concern you."

"How could you just steal someone else's work and pass it off as your own? This must be illegal. Vera's book is copyrighted."

Marla grabbed Alex and pulled her inside. "For God's sake, come in out of the hallway. You don't need to tell everyone in the hotel that you think what I did is illegal." Alex took another step inside.

Marla folded her arms across her chest. "You don't know the first thing about what's legal or illegal in book publishing."

"Well, enlighten me."

"Not that I need to explain this to you, but, first of all, you can't copyright a title, and hundreds of cover art is available over the Internet for anyone's use. You see books all the time with the same generic artwork or photograph."

148

"Marla, you used the *same story*, the *same* characters, everything, almost word for word!!"

Marla sighed deeply as though bored with the conversation. "Haven't you heard the expression, 'There's nothing new under the sun?' That's in the Old Testament. If you want to get all technical about it, Vera Blaze's story is a rip-off of Stephen King's, *Misery,* where a deranged fan holds her favorite author prisoner. There are only a limited number of stories, and then there are countless variations.

She looked up at the ceiling. "*West Side Story* is a remake of *Romeo and Juliet.* Shall I go on?"

"So, did you tell Vera you had written a 'variation' of her book?"

"No, it wasn't necessary. Vera had a good idea, but I could have thought of it. I used it and wrote a better book. Also, I have the bigger platform to sell it. My books have a name publisher, and she's self-published. What I did might be construed as plagiarism, which may be a breach of ethics to some, but it's not illegal. Look it up. You'll find that it's not a crime. Now, if that's all –"

"Not quite. I intend to show your 'variation' to Vera."

"I wouldn't do that."

"I know. I am. She has a right to know about this and to pursue whatever recourse is available to her. Since a title can't be copyrighted, maybe she should retitle hers *Screaming Bloody Murder.* She might get more sales when her book is ordered online, being mistaken for yours."

"You better not get involved with this, Alex. Like I said in the beginning, it's none of your business."

"I'm sorry, Marla. I wasn't trying to dig up something on you. I just happened to find this, and now I can't look the other way. I have a feeling you've done this before this and since then, but I won't investigate. And if your rewrite of this book is only unethical as you say, nothing more will come of it."

Alex turned to leave. "I have to get ready for our dinner cruise. I hope you're coming, too. I will promise you one thing. I won't mention this to the others. I don't think it's my job to ruin your reputation. I'll leave that for you to do."

Chapter 24

A HALF HOUR LATER, Alex was looking over her wardrobe to find something to wear on the cruise. Since she would be out on the water in the evening, she had to put on something for warmth. Her other consideration, she had to admit, was that she wanted to wear something flattering. Not that she was interested in inviting male attention, but it was gratifying that a handsome man like Matthew found her attractive. At least, Flossie thought that was the case. And, really, what was the harm in trying to look good?

She stepped into her long paisley skirt and pulled her fitted white sweater over her head. After pushing her feet into high-heeled sandals, and draping a long shell necklace over her head, she glanced approvingly at herself in the mirror. She'd let her hair hang loose, as it would be impossible to control it out on the water, anyway.

Just after five o'clock, she stood on the dock waiting for her group to arrive. So far, only Virgil Meade had boarded the catamaran. Looking through the crowd on the pier, she picked out Flossie, Cynthia and Adeline coming, all dressed in various bright-colored floral prints.

As they approached her, Flossie stretched out her arms. "Alex, you look beautiful – all dressed up for a special evening, I see." She winked, knowingly.

Alex made a face. "Flossie, you never give up. You ladies can get on board if you want to hold a few seats in the dining room. Here are your tickets. I'll be the last one on. See you inside."

A couple minutes later Ethan and Joan O'Leary came along. Joan said, "Good call to arrange for a dinner cruise. Two of our favorite activities combined – eating and boating.

"Thanks. I thought it would be a shame to come to Key West and not go out on the gulf. This outfit serves good food, too, unlike some who figure that people won't notice if the food is bad since it's so nice to be out on the water."

"We've been on dinner cruises like that before," Ethan said. "It's true that one accepts a lower standard of dining on a boat. Most people are there primarily for the cruising. Having anything to eat is like a bonus."

"Well, I think you'll be pleased with this operation. Here are your boarding passes. I'll see you inside in a few minutes."

Turning back, she saw Matthew Evans and Jack Burns making their way through the crowd. Matthew looked nautical in a light blue shirt, carrying a navy sports coat hooked over his thumb, while Jack had on his usual windbreaker and khakis.

"Alex, you look pretty hot tonight," Jack commented, ogling her.

Matthew elbowed him in the ribs. "Show some respect, Jack." In a theatrical aside to Alex he said, "Don't worry about him. He's really harmless."

"I'm not worried," Alex said, airily. "I have his ticket for the free bar." She fanned the boarding passes in front of them.

"Hah! Good one. I like the way you put Jack in his place."

She gave a little shrug. "Actually, we need both you guys around to dance with, so don't go too far away."

Jack smirked. "See, smartass? Alex wants my body."

He patted her on the shoulder. "Kidding. I'll be happy to oblige. And I'll be a gentleman. You've got Ethan and Virgil, too, although I doubt that Virgil can dance the salsa."

"Neither can you," Matthew said dryly.

"Good point."

Alex noticed another guest approaching, just then. "Oh, excuse me, Matthew ... Jack ... I'd like you to meet John Austin. I invited him to join us. You probably don't recognize John, but he's the actor who impersonates Marilyn Monroe at the club next door."

"No. Seriously?" Jack said, taken aback. "You do a helluva job, man, and I'm old enough to remember the real Marilyn Monroe. There's never been an actress like her since. She was positively luminous."

"I've loved her in her movies," Matthew commented. "And I have to agree with Jack about her beauty, and your uncanny performance. It's a really good show, man. Sorry about that Fonda Dix, the comedian who died."

John lowered his eyes. "Paul Robbins was his real name. He was my partner. Alex has urged me to have his death investigated because John didn't have heart disease, making his death suspicious. The ME performed an autopsy today, so we should have an answer tomorrow about what really killed him, if it wasn't just a heart attack.

"Anyway, I don't need to go into all of that. And I didn't mean to get all morbid, here. Alex asked me to come along to have a little fun. She's become a friend."

"Our Alex seems to wear many hats," Jack commented, putting an arm around her. "And now we can add 'homicide detective' to the list."

Extending a hand to John he said, "Well, we're happy to have you, dude. C'mon, let's get on board. I'd like to have time for a drink before we have to eat. We seem to be always eating dinner while the sun's still shining. See ya later, Alex."

After they walked away, she checked her watch. Ten minutes to departure. Three women yet to arrive. Looking down the pier, she noticed there were several people hurrying to make the boat. As they got closer she caught sight of Frances and Grace behind them. Neither one looked like they were going to a party, as they plodded along in their drab clothes, staring at the ground.

"Hi, ladies," Alex chirped. "Glad you could make it."

Frances glared at her and held up a finger to her lips, followed by a curt nod towards Grace.

"Uh, well, this should be a good evening," Alex tried again.

Grace's eyes narrowed. "It hasn't been a good day."

"I'm sorry to hear that. Maybe getting out on the boat, having a good meal, and listening to some reggae music will make you feel better."

"I'll never feel better."

Alex sighed. "Didn't things go well with Lorna Green? It's not the end of the negotiations, is it?"

"I don't want to talk about it," she mumbled.

"Okay…I understand. Here are your passes. Why don't you get on board and find seats in the dining room. Most everyone is already up there. I'll see you on board."

Turning towards the pier, Alex noted that there were just a few stragglers left who were still making their way to the boat. The last one to finally saunter up was Marla Page, barely recognizable in outsized dark glasses and a long white scarf wrapped around her head like a hijab worn by a Muslim.

"Hi, Marla. Good to see you."

"Yeah…right. There was no one left at the hotel to eat with, so I didn't have much of a choice."

"Well, for whatever reason, I'm glad you decided to join us. Here's your boarding pass. We're the last two to get on. Like you thought, everyone else is here."

Alex kept a safe distance behind Marla walking up the gangplank. *I think I'll take Jack's lead and head for the bar. This looks like it could be a very long two-hour cruise.*

Chapter 25

AS THE CATAMARAN got underway, Alex felt heartened by the party atmosphere. Reggae music was being piped throughout the craft from the band playing on the main deck. The bouncy rhythm and the mellow notes perfectly complemented the soft breeze and the gentle roll of the boat.

She decided to first take in the view from the top deck. On her way to the open stairway at the end of the boat, she had to steady herself on the posts she passed. Mounting the stairs, she boosted herself up by grabbing onto the two handrails.

Once on top, she scanned the deck, but didn't see anyone she knew among the couple dozen people lining the railing. Most were on the city-side, gazing at the crowds on Mallory square and the city harbor. Of course, many people were there to wait for the sun to set in half an hour.

She headed over to a roofed structure at the opposite end of the deck that she assumed to be the bar.

To no surprise, Jack Burns was already ensconced in his preferred seat at one end and, as usual, he was holding forth on some favorite topic to a captivated audience. She was pleased to see that John Austin was there with Matthew.

As she walked up, Jack interrupted himself to greet her. "Oh, here's our lovely tour director, aka homicide detective. Want a drink Alex, or are you on official police business?"

She waved off his tease. "Just order me a strawberry daiquiri, Jack. You seem to be closest to the bartender, as usual."

She turned towards Matthew and John. "So, how's it going? The buffet is open downstairs now, if you want to eat before watching the sunset up here."

Matthew rolled his eyes towards Jack. "We'll have to see if we can pry 'the professor' off his barstool. He's been giving a lecture on 'Cuba before the revolution.' Someone told him he looks like Hemingway, and he went off from there."

John chuckled. "You were right when you said these are some interesting people." He leaned over and asked in a low voice. "Is Grace Tuttle here? Can you tell me what she looks like?"

Matthew stage-whispered back, "She has a beaver puppet on one hand. You can't miss her."

"No, no, no," Alex protested, reaching for the iced drink being handed to her. "She left Benny back in the room. She's not up here … and you probably won't see her near a bar, anyway. She has long brown hair held back in a low ponytail. And she has on a brown top with brown slacks."

"So, she looks like a beaver." John said, straight-faced.

"Almost exactly," Matthew put in, smirking. "She also has a major overbite."

"Matthew!" Alex tried not to smile as she turned back to John. "She's with her friend Frances, who's middle-aged with bright blue eyes –"

"Who carries around a demonic doll," Matthew finished.

She lightly punched him. "John, after I finish my drink I'm going to go down to the main deck to get something to eat. Whenever you come down, look for me and I'll introduce you to her and the others. She must be on the main deck. I saw her get on the boat."

Matthew frowned. "Uh, may I ask why John wants to meet Grace? Or is that none of my business?"

Alex shrugged, nonchalantly. "Oh, John had mentioned that Fonda Dix, er, Paul, had teased someone who had a beaver puppet. I told him that it was Grace, and he was curious to see who she was."

Matthew gave her the fish eye. "No…that's not it." He paused. "Wait a minute. You must think Grace had something to do with Fonda Dix's death that you thought was suspicious. Am I right?"

Her eyes widened in alarm. "Shhh! Seriously, Matthew, don't tell anybody that. It's a crazy idea, and I have no evidence, whatsoever. And it's totally unprofessional for me to spread an ugly rumor like that about someone in my own tour group, for Pete's sake."

Matthew waved a hand. "Don't worry, I won't say anything. But I was there at the club that night, so I know it's not an altogether 'crazy idea.'"

John took a sip of his beer. "Since you guessed that much, my plan to test Alex's theory is that I tell Grace about my relationship with Paul and see what kind of reaction I get."

Alex put down her glass. "John, I should warn you that Grace is in a foul mood tonight. Remember I said how excited she was that Disney had expressed

158

some interest in her stories? Well, something has gone very wrong. I don't know what."

As the three of them sat quietly for a moment listening to the music and sipping their drinks, they heard Jack's voice in the background. "A veteran correspondent told me he was at the Tropicana when Batista would come in with his bodyguards and then carry out a satchel of cash – it was protection money paid by Meyer Lansky so he could run his illegal activities outta the club. Batista got 10 mil a year from the mafia to let them operate their favorite businesses in Havana, like gambling, prostitution and drugs."

***

A FEW MINUTES LATER, Alex was in the main cabin carrying her dinner plate from the buffet table over to join Flossie and Cynthia, who were already on their desserts.

"How do you like the food?" Alex asked as she sat down. "Good, isn't it?

"It's delicious," Flossie answered.

Cynthia agreed. "Everything is fresh, and hot or cold, whichever it's supposed to be. You'll love the pineapple grilled chicken and deep fried plantains."

Alex took a couple of bites. Mmmm." Looking around she picked out several of the group in the room, at the buffet table, seated at the counter, and at one of the tables. "I don't see Grace and Frances. Have you seen them recently?"

Flossie threw up her hands. "Oh, those two! I waved at them to come and join us. I know they saw me, but they took off for the other end of the room, or the 'cabin,' or whatever they call this place. I don't know what's wrong with them."

159

Alex finished chewing her mouthful. "I know it didn't go well with the rep from Disney, but Grace didn't tell me what happened. I suppose we'll hear something eventually. Whatever happened apparently caught her off guard."

Over the next several minutes, Alex finished her dinner while chatting with the two women. The cabin had started emptying out as people headed up the stairs or out on the deck to observe the sunset.

Just as the three of them stood to leave, Matthew and John walked up. Alex briefly introduced John and steered them both in the other direction. "Apparently Grace and Frances went this way earlier. I don't see them, but there are a lot of people standing around. Let's go down there to the bar and I'll look around."

When they eased their way through the crowd, Alex was astonished to see Frances and Grace sitting on stools at one end of the bar. Getting John's attention, she pointed at them and headed their way.

When the two women saw her, she tried to act surprised. "Grace! Frances! I wondered where you two had gone to. Oh, I see you got another margarita, Grace."

Grace squinted her small eyes that were now bleary, as she tried to focus. "I've had more than one. It's a free bar, you know. I can have all I want. Frances here can't even keep up with me."

Frances sat there stonily, without looking up.

Alex kept her voice calm. "Grace, you seem to be taking it hard that it didn't go well with Lorna Green from Disney. What happened, anyway?"

"What happened is that she's a bitch – scuze my French. It seems she sent a picture of Benny to her 'legal department,' and they said that Benny is like their 'Bucky Beaver' that they trademarked, and that

160

I'm using him illegally for a commercial purpose or something. She said she hadn't known cuz he was trademarked in the 50s before she was born, and he hasn't been used since the 1970s. She said I was lucky they didn't sue me, but she said it more crudely than that."

Grace took a big gulp of her margarita. "You know what I've gone through to get that contract? No, of course you don't. You have no idea."

"Look I agree that it's extremely disappointing, Grace, but try to see it in perspective. You still have your books. Maybe you can get a different beaver, or another animal, even."

Grace raised her upper lip above her teeth. "You don't get it. Benny and I are in this together."

"Well, maybe you're right that I can't really understand. Anyway, I don't want to bother you any longer. We just came over to get a drink to take outside to catch the sunset." She half turned to indicate John and Matthew with her. "Oh, sorry. I should introduce you. This is John Austin. You've seen him before, but you probably don't realize it. You saw him when he was impersonating Marilyn Monroe at the 'Some Like It Hot.'"

Grace's jaw jutted out as she rounded on him. "Oh, yeah, I remember *you,* and your kind. You're all a bunch of sickos!"

"Grace, please!" Alex chastened her.

"That's uncalled for, Grace," Matthew added.

John lurched forward and got in her face. "We are all *talented artists* who work hard at our craft, and we don't deserve to be slandered by people like you who have a problem with who we are."

Grace drew herself up, and puffed out her chest. "I'm entitled to my opinion, and I say you're all abominations, especially that black queer, Fonda Dix. And what a disgusting name!"

His name was *Paul* and he was my partner and my best friend."

"Well, now he's your dead friend."

John grabbed her shirt. "Do you know something about that?"

Matthew caught hold of him. "Easy, man. It's not worth it."

"Well, do you?!" John demanded, his eyes bulging.

Grace twisted her mouth into a sneer. "You ain't got *nothin'* on me, and you *never will.*"

Alex yanked John backwards and took his place. "Grace, what do you mean by that? Did you have *anything* to do with Paul's death?"

Grace's head lolled over to one side. "I wouldn't touch that freak, and I don't appreciate this homo putting his hands on me, neither. Now, leave me alone." She turned away and chugged down the rest of her drink.

Friday morning

Chapter 26

ALEX JUMPED OUT OF BED the next morning, her mind racing with plans to work on unresolved issues in the morning, and to prepare for Arlie's arrival in the afternoon. This was the last day of the seminar, the final push for the authors to sell books to make the trip profitable, and the last opportunity they had to attend the panel discussions and lectures that were the focus of the four-day festival.

Dominating her thoughts was the continuing question of whether or not Grace was somehow responsible for the death of Paul Robbins. After the woman's drunken rant last night condemning Paul and the other female impersonators as being perverse and evil, Alex was more suspicious of her than ever. And, even if she wasn't guilty of actual murder, her verbal attack had definitely killed the mood of the evening.

Thinking back, Alex cringed at the absurdity that her paramount concern before the cruise was that there wouldn't be enough dance partners to go around.

After talking to Grace for five minutes, the last thing on her mind was dancing; kick boxing, maybe, but not dancing.

Fortunately, the others in the group had been spared Grace's vitriol and were thoroughly enjoying themselves in the spirit of the occasion.

Jack Burns, true to his word, had come down to the main cabin and danced with several of the women, even managing some creditable Latin dance steps to the beat of the band's reggae music.

Sitting by and observing, Alex couldn't help but feel cheered by the dancing, the up-tempo songs, and the festive atmosphere created by the lighted dance floor and the mirrored disco ball overhead.

But when the cruise ended back at the harbor, she was reminded that she had to clear up several problems before Arlie arrived and they started on what had been planned as a carefree, fun weekend.

Before disembarking, she had asked John Austin to let her know the results of the autopsy as soon as he heard. Hopefully, the Medical Examiner would make a determination of death by natural causes, which would at least eliminate Grace as a murder suspect. The woman would still be disruptive neurotics, but Alex could live with that.

She felt sorry for poor John having taken the brunt of Grace's rage. Of course, much of her anger was misplaced as it was due to losing the Disney deal and having her blessed beaver puppet being cited for trademark infringement.

Thinking of that reminded Alex that she had to alert Vera Blaze to Marla's copyright violation of her book, *Screams in the Night,* by showing her Marla's, *Screaming Bloody Murder*. She couldn't even imagine Vera's shock and distress upon learning that her book, which had probably taken her many months to write, had been lifted in its entirety by Marla, who stole not only her entire creation, but the income from all the sales that should have been hers.

It would be a challenging day of dealing with tough situations, but her reward would be to fulfill her responsibilities, and later, to welcome Arlie for the weekend. Catching sight of herself in the dresser mirror, she was reminded that she had better shower and dress so that she could get on with what she had to do.

***

A HALF HOUR LATER, she was making her way to the elevator wearing her favorite navy blue knit top with white capris, and carrying her large tan bag over her shoulder. The white pants might have been a mistake to try to keep clean for a whole day, but she'd try to be careful.

On the ride down, she was backed up against the wall, as usual, but held her purse in front to give herself a little more room until the passengers started exiting on the ground level.

Walking past the lobby, she glanced in looking for John, but didn't see him. Likewise, when she looked around the dining room, she didn't see him, or anyone from her group. Choosing one of the smaller tables, she sat by herself, facing the doorway.

While sipping her second cup of coffee and mentally rehearsing what she would say to Vera Blaze, she saw John Austin coming in. Signaling to him, he returned her wave and crossed the room to join her.

"I was hoping I'd find you here by yourself," he said in a rush. "I had called up to your room, and when there was no answer, I figured you had come down here early."

165

"Why, did you hear something? Wait – don't tell me yet. Let's get you a cup of coffee. Here's my waitress with the coffee pot."

After the server left with John's order, he leaned forward, resting his elbows on the table. "I just heard from the doctor who talked to the Medical Examiner. First, he told me all the things he *didn't* find− you know how doctors are. They have to be thorough and explain everything."

Alex nodded. "Yeah, but it's a good things to get all the details. So, tell me, what didn't the ME find?"

"Well, first off and most interesting, there were no signs of heart disease. The heart was of normal size, and there weren't any blockages he could see."

"Wow. That's pretty significant, considering everyone agreed he died of a heart attack. So, did the ME eliminate natural causes?" Her look was intense with anxiety.

John shook his head. "Not so fast. Let me go through it with you like the doctor did with me, so you know everything I know."

He looked down at a sheet of paper he was unfolding. "One second, let me check my notes. Okay, the ME tested for all the poisons and their byproducts you thought might have been used."

Alex's face lit up. "Really? Then he thought my hunches had some merit?"

"Yeah … but it turns out they didn't."

"Oh."

"But the doctor said it was good to eliminate substances like, let me see here, 'Ethylene glycol,' 'succynocholine,' and 'pentobarbital.'"

She ticked them off on her fingers and paused, her brow furrowed in thought. Then her face cleared. "Oh, so I was right. It was potassium chloride!" she said out loud before she realized that she could be heard two tables over. "I mean, was that it?" she asked in a hoarse whisper.

"No, although that was a good guess, the doctor said, because it can cause a fatal heart attack without being detected 'postmortem,' as he put it."

"So, what *did* he find?" Her eyes widened.

"Well, remember I told you that one reason the ME wanted to do the autopsy was because he found a couple of puncture marks?"

"Yes, of course. Where were they?"

"Well, that's what was unusual. The two needle marks were in the chest area somewhere. I think the doctor identified a place between certain muscles or whatever. I didn't get that written down."

Alex waved away his concern. "That's all right. I wouldn't know, anyway. But, was he able to discover what drug or poison was injected there?"

"No. That's the problem. He couldn't detect any drug or poison he knew to test for."

Her face fell. "So, that's it? All he could find out was what was *not* there, and not what *was* there?"

"Nooo ... that's not all. I told you about all his tests and the placement of the needle marks to explain why he had to go to extraordinary lengths to look beyond the usual, if you can refer to drugs and poisons as 'usual.' The marks weren't in a place where addicts inject heroin, or where a diabetic would inject insulin.

"Okay, okay. I've got that. So?"

He held up a finger. "So, after examining the condition of the heart, testing for drugs and poisons, he performed what is called computed tomography, or CT."

"What's that for?"

"As I understand it, a CT is a precise test used to detect gas in coronary arteries or veins."

167

"Gas?"

"Well, it's really 'air,' but they refer to it as 'gas.' The doctor explained that if a large air bubble travels to the heart, it can cause a heart attack."

Alex looked confused. "So, Paul died from an air bubble in an artery? For sure?"

"Right. The ME could see it with the CT. He's positive, Alex."

"Could that have occurred naturally?"

John shook his head. "The ME makes a connection between the air bubble and the needle marks, which means the heart attack was induced."

"And that means–"

"That means it was *murder*, Alex. Just as you said."

Friday morning

Chapter 27

I KNEW IT! I KNEW IT! Her voice was loud inside her head as she made her way down Duval Street. *I knew it was murder, but how can I connect the injection of an air bubble with Grace?*

As she thought about it, she had to concede that Grace could never have been alone with the man, and even if she had been, he wouldn't have stood still for her shooting an empty vial into him. According to the doctor, that's how the air bubble was delivered. So, the evidence from the autopsy seemed to point away from Grace, even though she was the most likely candidate that Alex knew about.

At least she was right that Paul had been murdered. John Austin appreciated that that had been established, even though it raised more questions than it answered. As she had told him at breakfast, he would have to go back over Paul's movements from the day before through the hours before he collapsed in the lobby to see who had access to him.

Then it occurred to her. *John* was the only person who was with Paul right before he died. *He* would be the one the police would suspect and investigate. But it was hard to believe that John's grief hadn't been genuine, or that he could be capable of killing his partner that he loved. Or *said* he loved. Maybe he was grieving because he had done such a terrible thing in the heat of anger. Hold on. You don't shoot an air bubble into someone during an argument. And how would he know how to do it? John's an actor, not a doctor. He said he couldn't even remember the name of the site of the injection.

Wait a minute – what did she just say to herself? *John is an actor.* The man makes people believe that he's Marilyn Monroe, for Pete's sake. He could be putting on an act for her.

Oh, this was too much to think about right now. She felt a headache coming on. She'd have to think through the whole matter later – it wasn't making any sense to her right now, anyway.

Besides, she was coming up to the San Carlos Institute. She unconsciously patted her purse with Marla's book inside that she would soon be showing to Vera Blaze.

What a morning she was having – first, a tête-à-tête about murder with John over breakfast, and now, a tête-à-tête about larceny with Vera before lunch.

Stepping inside the building, she looked around the anteroom for any sign of OPAL people she wanted to avoid right now. She definitely had to dodge Marla Page. She had been lucky not to have seen the woman since confronting her about her thievery. She checked behind her to make sure that she wasn't being followed.

Maybe this was just one book of many that Marla had ripped off. So, it was no big deal, Alex thought.

170

Retracing her steps of yesterday afternoon, she located the far room where she had come upon Vera Blaze. Entering it, she immediately spotted the woman standing behind her table against the back wall. She was immediately recognizable by the white streak in her hair. Fortunately, there weren't any customers in the area so she could speak privately.

Hesitating momentarily, she swallowed hard and took a deep breath before walking over to Vera's table.

"Oh, hi!" Vera greeted her as she approached. "I remember you from yesterday. Your, um, fluffy hair is distinctive," she added by way of explanation.

Alex chuckled. "Funny, I remembered you by *your* hair. And 'fluffy' is a much nicer word than 'frizzy,' so thanks for that.

"Unfortunately, I'm not here to exchange pleasantries − or even to buy another book."

Vera's smile faded. "Oh...o-kay. What is it? Was something wrong with the book you bought? If there was, I'd be happy to exchange it."

"No, no. There was nothing wrong with your book. In fact, I want to compliment you on writing such a suspenseful page-turner. I really enjoyed it. But my coming back to see you has to do with another book." Vera's forehead was now creased in confusion.

"Let me explain. My name is Alex Trotter and I'm a tour director from Chicago. I'm here escorting a group of writers from the Oak Park Authors League who are attending the book festival.

"O-kay. So, what does that have to do with me?"

"Good question. That leads me right into what I need to tell you...that I've been dreading to tell you since I made the discovery yesterday afternoon. The best way to explain it is to show you this book written by Marla Page, one of the authors in my tour group." Alex pulled out her copy of *Screaming Bloody Murder* from her purse and handed it to Vera.

Her eyebrows rose in surprise. "Oh, she used the same Edvard Munch painting I used. That's all right. It's an image that anyone can use now." Her facial muscles relaxed.

"That's not it, Vera." Alex took another deep breath. "Read the back."

Vera turned the book over and quickly scanned the text, blinking in disbelief. "What?! This is *my* synopsis, almost verbatim! I don't understand … what is this?" She held it out to Alex.

"Look inside, Vera. I had this book in my room and compared it page by page with yours after I got back yesterday. The characters, the story line, everything is the same except for slightly different wording."

Vera skimmed down a couple of pages. "I can't believe it! This is *my* book. But I didn't steal it from *her*, if that's what you thought."

"Oh, no, Vera. I know that. Look at the copyright date on Marla's *Screaming Bloody Murder*. It was published only a couple months ago, and by a well-known publisher, as you can see. You self-published your book three years ago. There's no question of *who* violated *who's* copyright."

"But I don't understand. Why would she duplicate my book? She's an author, right? Why doesn't she just write her own books?"

"That's another good question. I don't know whether she always does this, or what. She had told me that she's a best-selling author, which I don't doubt with the marketing and reputation of Kensingham publishing behind her. And I know that since you're self-published you don't have those same advantages."

Vera made a little guttural sound. "You've got that right. That's why I'm here at the festival. I go to all the fairs that look promising, as well as visiting book stores, gift shops, drug stores, any place that might be willing to display and sell my books. Even so, I'm lucky if I sell a couple hundred books a year. I'm not making a living at this, but I can't afford to have my writing cost me a lot, either."

Alex shook her head, sympathetically. "Well, I think you can make some real money out of this situation if you go to a copyright attorney and sue Marla. She's already admitted to me that she used your book to write hers. As soon as I read through the two books to be sure, I confronted her with the evidence."

"You did? What did she have to say for herself?"

"At first she was shocked. Then she tried to be nonchalant about the whole thing. Tried telling me that there are only so many stories in the world, and that authors merely write their own variations. She had the nerve to tell me that she wrote your story better than you did, if you can believe that."

Vera held her head in her hands. "Oh, my God! Let me see this again!" She cracked opened the book, flipped through several pages, running her finger down the middle of each one.

"Hunh! Better than mine? She just rearranged the wording a little, but all the thoughts and actions of the characters are the same, from what I just read." She held out the book to her, but Alex pushed it back.

"No, this is yours so you can go over it carefully and then give it to an attorney. You can't let Marla Page get by with not only stealing your story, but earning money from it that should have been yours."

Vera's eyes got misty. "What you don't know is that this really *is* my story. Oh, not that my sorority sisters came running when I called for help, and that they held my rapist captive. Actually, when I was raped at the party, I didn't scream at all.

"I was a naïve little freshman who was still a virgin. I drank at the party, and willingly went into the lounge with that boy because he was cute and popular. And after he raped me, I felt like it was my fault – that I had asked for it.

"Afterwards, I never reported the incident. It took me years to get over it, if I ever did. That's why I wrote the book – my first book. It was cathartic for me to get my revenge out on the printed page.

"There are lots of factual details in the book, so I thought maybe my rapist would read it and recognize himself, and see what could have happened to him. I hope that the end of the book showed that I'm a strong woman today."

Her jaw tightened. "This Marla Page stole the wrong book from the wrong author. I'll be damned if I'm going to be raped *twice* and not get justice."

Vera took Alex's hand in both of hers. "I can't thank you enough for this. It may be difficult and expensive to hire an attorney and go through all the legal wrangling. I don't know much about all this, but I will try.

"I'm staying at the Sunset Inn until Sunday if you learn anything else about Marla Page I should know. Here's my card."

Alex took it and slipped it into her purse. "Good. I'll email you Marla's contact info. I'm at the Cest' La Vie through the weekend. Who knows? Maybe Marla will want to clear her conscience and settle out of court.

"I don't know much about copyright laws, but this would have to be an open-and-shut case. And if can use another literary metaphor, I'd say that any judge who hears your whole story will want to throw the book at her." She grinned sheepishly. "That was pretty bad, huh?"

Friday afternoon

Chapter 28

AT A QUARTER AFTER FOUR, Alex sat fidgeting in the lobby of the inn as she waited for Arlie to arrive from the airport. His plane from Jacksonville would have landed by now, so it shouldn't be long. Although she and Arlie had a comfortable, caring relationship, it was a long-distance one, so she was always a little insecure about first seeing him after a separation.

This time, she had seen him less than a month ago at Christmastime. The tension she felt today had more to do with just learning that Fonda Dix had definitely been murdered, which had not only confirmed her belief, but had renewed her suspicion about Grace.

Arlie was anticipating a carefree weekend with her, and she owed it to him to be cheerful and attentive. After all, she had asked him to fly out for what she had described as a laid-back party atmosphere in Key West. He didn't anticipate being drawn into some murder investigation because she suspected that a member of her tour group was involved. That had happened twice before, she reminded herself. It might be getting a little old. Besides, the police were undoubtedly investigating the case now. They didn't want someone to get away with murder, either.

Just then she noticed that the front door was cracked open, bringing her back to the present. Jumping up, she looked expectantly at the widening gap until she could see that it was Marla Page coming in, pushing open the door with the heft of her two canvas bags of books.

As she came into the lobby, she caught sight of Alex watching her, and glared back without speaking.

"Hello, Marla."

"Don't tell me you're waiting for me, Alex. What do you want to accuse me of now?"

"Actually, I'm waiting for my boyfriend. Remember, the homicide detective I mentioned to you at Flossie's tea? But I did knock on your door earlier when you weren't there. I wanted to tell you that I went to see Vera Blaze this morning. I took her your book, *Screaming Bloody Murder.* Needless to say she was very upset."

"Then don't say it."

"Funny. Anyway, I felt I owed it to Vera to tell her about you stealing her book. And I thought I should let you know that I did. I'm sure she'll be pursuing the matter in court. As I said before, I'm not taking this any further, myself."

Marla's face reddened. "I wrote a *variation* on her story about a girl being raped. Hardly a new subject!" she sputtered before turning on her heel and trudging off,   dragging her bags.

Alex shook her head as she watched the woman disappear through the hallway door.

With a sigh she walked across the room to look out the window. Flossie, Cynthia, Adeline and Virgil were just getting out of a cab. They also appeared to be weighed down by canvas bags containing unsold books.

After Alex had seen Vera Blaze, she had stopped by the OPAL table and helped them take down signs and get organized before she returned to the hotel to get ready for Arlie. Closing down at the end of the festival had been made easier by the seminar committee that asked the authors to only be responsible for removing their personal belongings. The clean-up crews would be taking down the tables and chairs and carting them away. And, after the authors had all left the area, the crews would also clean up and haul away the tons of litter left behind by the thousands of people who had attended the event.

Alex hurried over to open the door as the foursome lurched in with their burdens.

"Oh, thank you, dear," Flossie gushed, putting down her bags right inside the door. "I don't know why I keep doing these seminars. Except that I love signing and selling my books, and talking to people, while making a little money to boot."

Alex chuckled. "Sounds like you have some pretty good reasons. How did you all do? I see you didn't sell all of your books, but did you do as well as you expected?"

Cynthia and Adeline answered that it had been a good crowd for romances as there were so many women who attended.

Virgil heavily set down his two bags before he stood and slowly pulled back his shoulders to relieve the apparent strain. "I'm afraid I can't echo these ladies' positive assessment of a receptive crowd with regard to sales of *my* volumes of metered verse."

Alex considered his remarks. "So you didn't do as well as you had hoped."

"I would answer you with a qualified affirmative response, in that I sold approximately as many tomes as my projection had indicated."

Alex took another stab. "So, you did as well as you had predicted."

Just then their attention was drawn to the front door as it swung open. Alex looked over expectantly; but it wasn't Arlie who came in. Jack Burns could be seen outside holding the door open as Matthew Evans, Ethan O'Leary and Joan staggered in with their bags of books.

"Well, hello, folks," Jack said as he followed them in, surprised at the welcoming committee.

"We were just comparing notes on the seminar," Flossie offered. "Most of us were very satisfied with our sales and thought it was a most agreeable crowd. How about all of you?"

Ethan answered, "I did well enough. But I learned long ago that science fiction only sells well to niche audiences, like at a convention on the subject."

"But we've enjoyed being here for many other reasons," Joan added. "And I'm looking forward to getting out and sightseeing some more tomorrow."

"Oh, good," Alex said. "I've got a couple of stops lined up for the morning, and some ideas for the afternoon. My ... uh ... friend Arlie Tate will be joining us. Soon, actually. I'm just waiting for him to come from the airport."

Cynthia's face lit up. "You have a boyfriend coming? How exciting! I bet he's a rich, handsome stockbroker or something."

"He's a policeman," Flossie replied dryly.

"Homicide detective," Alex corrected her.

The front door quietly opened without anyone's notice.

"Alex?" a male voice called.

Everyone turned towards the speaker in the doorway. Hearing the familiar voice, Alex tried in vain to see around the O'Learys, Flossie and Cynthia who were blocking her view. "Arlie," she called out, trying to make her way towards the door, needing first to turn sideways to ease herself between Ethan and Joan, only to find herself blocked by Matthew and Jack. "Uh, excuse me." The two men stepped back a few inches.

Eight pairs of eyes then turned to gape at the man with the full brows, keen eyes and tousled sandy-colored hair who stood by the door. Arlie looked curiously back at them as Alex came squirting through the crowd into a clearing to get up next to him.

Arlie smiled at her, bewildered. "Hi, babe. Am I interrupting something?"

Alex waved her hands in protest. "No, no, of course not." Half-turning she added, "These are some of the authors in my tour group. The seminar just ended so they all came back to the hotel at about the same time."

She hurriedly made all the introductions as everyone responded with appropriate words of welcome. As she concluded introductions with Matthew and Jack, she glanced around the group. "I hope that you'll all get to know Arlie over the next couple of days, but please excuse us now. I'm sure he wants to catch his breath and get settled a little after his trip.

"As I had told you earlier, you're on your own for dinner tonight, so you can pick your own restaurant. We'll meet together for breakfast tomorrow in the dining room. Maybe shoot for eight o'clock, okay?"

Hearing expressions of agreement, she tugged at Arlie's elbow and pulled him across the lobby towards the elevator hallway.

"That wasn't the way I planned to welcome you to Key West," she said under her breath as they heade3d towards the elevator.

"Well, I'm glad to hear that," Arlie drawled. "I thought you could do a little better than jumping out from behind a crowd of people."

The elevator door opened, and three women came out. Alex and Arlie stepped in as the only passengers to go up.

Pressing the button she said, "I know this isn't much of an elevator, but the stairs are even worse. We're on the 3rd floor, so it'll take a while, too. What this elevator lacks in size, it doesn't make up for in speed."

As the door closed, he let his carry-on slide to the floor before putting his arms around her and tenderly, but firmly, kissing her. "That's *my* version of a greeting," he whispered hoarsely in her ear.

"That was *so* much better than mine. Of course I had an audience with me, as you pointed out." Glancing up over his shoulder she said, "Oh, wait a minute. I almost forgot, there's a camera mounted up there in the corner, filming us."

"So? I only *kissed* you, Alex. I didn't rob you."

"Right." She wrinkled up her forehead. "Is it usual to have a surveillance camera in a hotel elevator?"

"Sure. And it's perfectly legal. Hotels have a right to make a record of everyone who has access to its floors. But it's for video only; no sound. They can't record people's words without their permission."

He raised one eyebrow and leered at her as he held her by the shoulders. "So ... I can describe what

I'm planning on doing to you in a few minutes, and they'll never know."

She feigned embarrassment and tried to match his Southern accent. "Why, Arlie Tate. I do declare, you're making me blush." Dropping the affectation she said, "Seriously, Arlie, about that camera. I'm wondering if there could be a videotape of someone who didn't belong in the hotel at the time I think someone was attacked who later died."

"Is this about that guy who had a heart attack?"

"You remembered! You probably want to know what happened about that."

"Not really." He twisted a lock of her hair around a finger. "Look, you can tell me all about it at dinner, but we have a better things to do with our time right now, don't we? I'm here to relax and have some fun, right?"

"Of course. I want that too. Just give me some time at dinner to give you an update. I think you'll be interested in what I have to say. Oh, here's our floor."

Starting down the hall she continued, "I hope you like our room. It's painted a shell pink. I mean, I think it's pretty, but it's not −"

"I wouldn't worry about it, babe. I don't plan to spend a lot of time staring at the walls."

Friday evening

Chapter 29

THE SKY WAS ROSY as Arlie and Alex were shown to their candlelit table on the roof level of the Top of the Key restaurant.

After clinking their margarita glasses to toast the weekend, Alex asked, "So, what do you think of this place? I chose this as the most romantic setting I knew for your first evening here. Here we have a spectacular view of the Gulf. We can watch the sun set over the water, and we'll be eating under the stars. While there's still a little light, you can look out over the railing and see the Old Town business district."

He rested his chin on his hands. "All true. And yet ... here I am gazing only at you. Hey, that even rhymes."

"Oh, please, Arlie. Flowery language doesn't suit you. Besides, I've heard enough poetry from Virgil this week to last a lifetime."

"Okay, you're right. But, seriously. it *is* beautiful up here. And I love sharing all of this with you." He raised his glass to her again. "Great choice. Did you say you've been here before?"

"Actually, I was here just the other night with my group. I thought you'd like it as much as I did. By the way, speaking of my group, I didn't have a chance to ask you what you thought of the people you met. You met all of the nice ones."

He gazed into the distance. "Well, let me think. I was only with them for about two minutes, if you recall. I dunno, they seemed pleasant enough. Oh, I remember what I wanted to ask you. Who was that aristocratic-looking older lady in the wire-rimmed glasses?"

She asked, "In the beige knit outfit?"

He nodded.

"Oh, she's my favorite. Flossie Quill. I'm probably closest to her in the group. What about her?"

"She gave me the stink eye when you introduced us, so I wondered what you'd told her about me."

"Ha. Ha. Nothing bad, I assure you. But I will confess the reason she might not have welcomed you with open arms. First of all, she's a Romance writer, and apparently likes to play matchmaker. And ever since I met her, she's been trying to fix me up with Matthew Evans."

Arlie rubbed his chin. "Was he the pale, balding guy who wears his pants above his waist?"

Alex snapped her napkin at him. "Nooo, smart-ass. That was Virgil Meade. Matthew was the tanned, handsome guy with dark hair who was wearing cream-colored tailored slacks."

"Not that you were paying a lot of attention," Arlie smirked.

"Oh, you know I'm just being snotty. Matthew's a nice enough guy. You'd like him if you got to know him. Flossie is the one who thinks he's God's gift – to me, in particular. I keep telling her that I'm spoken for.

"But she thinks Matthew is perfect for me because he's well-traveled, well-spoken, and is an artist as well as a writer."

"And I'm just a cop."

"Arlie, you're intelligent, and clever, and level-headed. You're the perfect yin to my yang – or the other way around; I never get it right. Anyway, we're good together, and I'm not looking to replace you.

"I should tell you, though, that I did have a drink with Matthew one night. I mean, just the two of us. We discovered that we both went to the Art Institute, so we got together to share some stories about our time there. That's all. It was hardly a date. Of course Flossie thinks any time the man comes near me he's showing a romantic interest in me. Believe me, I haven't encouraged him."

"No, of course not."

"I *haven't*, Arlie. Matthew seems to like me, but probably because I'm the only single woman his age on the tour." She took a sip of her drink and coyly peered over the edge.

"That makes sense," he shrugged, breaking a breadstick and dabbing butter on one end.

Opening her eyes wide, she shot back, "You're pretty quick to agree with that. It is *possible* that he finds me attractive and appealing, you know. Stranger things have happened."

Arlie reached over and stroked her cheek. "I think you're beautiful, but just as you started talking, your friend Matthew came in with a male companion that he seems to be pretty cozy with."

Her mouth dropped open. "What? Where?"

"Near the railing at my two o'clock. You can turn and look. They're concentrating on each other. They won't notice you. Besides, why shouldn't you see him?"

"It's just something unexpected, that's all." She started slowly rotating her head and shoulders together like she was wearing a neck brace.

"Just turn around, Alex. They're only looking at each other; not over at us."

She tossed down her napkin, bent over to pick it up and sneaked a glimpse at where Arlie had said the two men were sitting. Coming back up, she dramatically mouthed, "He's with John Austin."

"Alex, they can't hear you. Hell, I can't even hear you. Who's John Oster?"

"Austin. He's Fonda Dix's partner. Paul Robbins. You know, the man who died of a heart attack."

"Oh, okay. Gotcha. So, how does Matthew know this John Austin?"

"I got them together, I guess. Well, let me start from where I left off when I was talking with you on the phone. A lot has happened since then."

For the next several minutes she related what John had told her about Paul's death, starting with the discovery of the needle marks, moving through the findings of the autopsy, including the drugs that had been ruled out, and ending with the CT test that had revealed the arterial gas embolism that had been injected into Paul to stop his heart.

Finally, she told him about Grace's outburst with John on the dinner cruise when she was drinking far more than she was used to.

After Alex had finished, she leaned back in her chair to catch her breath, just as the waiter brought over their fresh grilled scallops.

"This looks delicious," she said, her eyes opening wide as she sat up.

"It does," he agreed. "Smells good, too. But, back to your story, I have to admit that I didn't see that coming. You were right all along, then. If it hadn't been for you, someone would have gotten away with murder."

"They still may," she said, taking a small forkful of basmati rice.

"Have you heard anything about the police investigation?"

"No, if there is one. As far as I know, Grace is the only person who could have wanted him dead because he mocked her and then got a 'Benny' for his act. The police wouldn't know anything about her and her connection with Paul. But, besides Grace, the only person I could think of as being a suspect is John. He's the only one who was with Paul before he had chest pains and died."

Arlie frowned as he touched his napkin to his mouth. "I doubt that John had anything to do with it. He was the one who made sure an autopsy was done after you questioned how his friend could have died by natural causes. He was even ready to pay for an independent one. Unless he's dumb as a rock, he would have had to have known that the needle marks would be seen, and that the gas embolism would be discovered with an autopsy. Everyone watches CSI, y'know."

"Oh, you're right, Arlie. I hadn't thought about that. I knew that it didn't make sense, but I hadn't figured out why. See how smart you are?"

"I didn't say I wasn't. That was your friend, Flossie."

"She didn't say that … exactly. Anyway, tomorrow you'll see Grace and her friend, Frances. With your powers of observation, you may detect something significant. There's something nagging me in the back of my mind, but I can't pull it up."

Arlie made a point of looking at his watch. "Okay, we've talked about Paul and John and Matthew and God-knows-who-else for at least half an hour, so I've lived up to my word. It's great that your instincts were correct, and Paul's death will be investigated as a murder, but now it's out of your hands.

"Look at where we are. As you pointed out, it's really romantic here, so let's not waste it. It's getting dark, the lights are coming on, and there's island music coming from down below. Oh, and we're across the street from the Gulf of Mexico. What else could we want?

"I say let's share a rich dessert, and go for a walk on the beach. Then, maybe stop in one of the clubs and have a drink before going back to the room. That's when the romantic part of the evening will really kick in, I promise you. How does that sound? Are you up for all that? Huh?" He picked up her hand and gently kissed her fingertips.

Alex sighed. "You really know how to turn on the charm, Arlie Tate. You never fail to surprise me… in a good way. Yes, of course I'm 'up for all that.' And I promise I won't say anything more about the people in my group, or who is a suspect, or who has a motive until tomorrow."

Saturday morning

Chapter 30

THE NEXT MORNING Alex stirred first, turning to smile at the sleeping Arlie as she thought back to their lovemaking the night before.

Looking ahead to the day, she vowed to herself to be discreet about probing any further into Paul Robbins' murder. Her primary role was as Arlie's companion, and to show him, and her group, the most important Key West tourist attractions in the little time they had left.

Easing out from between the sheets, she padded into the bathroom and closed the door to shower and get ready for the day. She needn't wake Arlie for a while as it wouldn't take him nearly as long to complete his morning routine. He only had to shower and shave before dressing. She had already plugged in her curling iron which was only the first step in the drawn-out process of transforming herself from being puffy-faced with snarled hair, to having smooth, even-toned skin, face-brightening make-up, and controlled, softly-curled hair.

After showering, she slipped into the yellow blouse, tan slacks and sandals she had worn on the first day. The color of her shirt set off her reddish hair, and the whole outfit was comfortable for sightseeing.

Back in the bedroom, she gently nudged Arlie into consciousness.

"Wha? Oh, hi, babe. Don't you look pretty. You put on a little lipstick, and you look perfect. I know I look like a bear in the morning.

"Thanks, but you don't know what I looked like twenty minutes ago."

"Well, I've gotta shave and shower just to look presentable. How much time do I have, anyway?"

"It's seven-thirty. I said we'd be in the dining room by eight. "I'm just going down now to check on something with the front desk. How about I meet you in the lobby, okay?"

"Sure. I'll be there on time. See you downstairs." He reached over and gave her a kiss on the cheek and stroked her hair. "It was great last night," he whispered.

***

RIDING DOWN IN THE ELEVATOR with three other people, she eyed the camera lens as she moved from one side to the other to see if she was always in view. As far as she could tell, the car was so small that the camera filmed the whole space.

After getting out, she walked over to the display rack in the hallway that contained brochures, picked out a few of them, and tucked them in her purse.

Then, she went into the lobby and headed for the front desk. Walking past the balding middle-aged male clerk, she approached the fresh-faced young woman at the other end who wore a, "Welcome, I'm Chrissie" name tag.

Placing her hands on the counter, Alex held eye contact with the clerk, "Hi, Chrissie. My name is Alex Trotter. I'm the owner of Globe-Trotter Travels, and I have a group staying here."

"Oh, yes. I've seen your company's name in our registry. How can I help you?"

"Well, one of my people may have been the victim of a pick-pocket here in the hotel this past Wednesday morning."

"Oh, my God!" Wide-eyed, Chrissie looked quickly to the left and right. "I think you should come back to the office to give me the details," she confided. "I wouldn't want to alarm our other guests. We don't really have any kind of *crime* here at the C'est La Vie."

As directed, Alex slipped around to a side door where she was admitted by the anxious clerk who showed her to the one chair in the office. The only other furniture in the cramped room was a filing cabinet and a desk, piled with papers, which Chrissie was leaning against.

"Okay, we can speak privately here," Chrissie said at a normal level. "So what happened, exactly?"

"Before I tell you what we know, let me assure you that my client does not hold the hotel responsible, nor does he want any compensation for the loss of his antique gold watch and chain."

Chrissie exhaled a stream of air, and crossed her legs. "I see. Well, then, how can I help you?"

"Well, since it's a valuable family heirloom, he'd like to know for sure whether it was dropped, or stolen. If it was stolen, he'll stop looking for it. He first missed it at breakfast on Wednesday. Of course, he's scoured his room and checked with your 'lost and found.'

"But, I'm hopeful that you have the tape of whatever the camera in the elevator recorded on Wednesday morning to know if someone stole it. People are really jammed into that elevator, so the watch could have been seen in his jacket pocket, and maybe was too much of a temptation for someone."

Chrissie had nodded thoughtfully through Alex's account, until she mentioned the tape. "So you're requesting that he see the tape?"

"Actually, *I'd* like to see the tape – for him. He's a shy poet who doesn't think anyone would steal from him. He's driving himself crazy trying to find it, but I think it had to have been stolen on the elevator, since he had it before he got on, and didn't have it when he got to the dining room five minutes later. It's very important to find an answer, even if we don't find the watch."

Chrissie glanced nervously at the closed door that led to the front desk. Speaking softly she said, "The problem is that the surveillance camera isn't for the use of our guests."

Alex smiled sweetly. "I know, it's to be used *against* your guests, it that were to become necessary. I'm sure that most of your guests have never even noticed the camera – which is as it should be," she added with a conspiratorial wink.

Chrissie jerked her thumb towards the door. "Mr. Hudson might not like me showing you the tape."

"Oh. Well, when does Mr. Hudson's shift end?"

Chrissie's face brightened. "This is his short day 'cuz he worked late last night! He should be gone by one. Can you come back after that? I don't see what it would hurt for you to see the tape, but there's no sense getting Mr. Hudson involved."

192

"No, we don't want that," Alex said, putting herself on Chrissie's side.

The clerk looked at her intently. "Are you absolutely sure you won't hold the hotel responsible if you find that there's been a theft? That would damage our reputation."

"I give you my word, Chrissie." She crossed her heart.

"Okay, I take you at your word. You can fast forward the tape to the time when your client gets on the elevator, and then it should take less than five minutes until he gets off. I guess no one here will ever be aware of you looking at it. I'll see you this afternoon, then. I'm here until five."

***

ALEX STEPPED OUT INTO the lobby just before the elevator door opened and Arlie walked out to join her.

"Hey, Arlie. Good timing."

"I hurried. Did you get what you needed?"

"No, but the clerk will have it this afternoon. I'll stop by and – oh, hell, I can't lie to you, Arlie. I arranged to see the videotape the elevator camera took on Wednesday morning, right before Paul Robbins had a heart attack."

He stopped and gave her a deadpan look.

"What?"

"I knew you were up to something. You're lousy at trying to throw me off the track, although I don't blame you for not waking me up with this half-baked scheme."

She made a pout. "Thanks. That videotape is the only recording of Fonda Dix before he collapsed in the lobby. That's what you call forensic evidence, my friend."

193

He made a little guttural sound. "Okay, okay. I'll never win an argument with you, anyway. Someone murdered Paul Robbins, and your guess is as good as anyone's."

"That's more like it. Let's go in for breakfast. After we eat I have sightseeing scheduled for the rest of the morning. We'll worry about the murder when we get back. Maybe we'll take in the arts and crafts show, too, if there's time."

Saturday morning

Chapter 31

ALEX MET WITH EVERYONE at breakfast to tell them about the guided tours of the Hemingway House and the Little White House that she had arranged for this morning. A bus would pick them up in front of the hotel at nine o'clock. She encouraged them all to take advantage of this opportunity as they were two must-see tourist attractions.

After the tour, they would be brought back to the hotel at around lunchtime, when they would be at leisure for the rest of the afternoon. From their location, they could easily explore the downtown area on foot.

One attraction in Old Town that weekend was a juried art show that included over a hundred artists from all over the country. Alex suggested it would be a good opportunity to pick up a special memento, choosing from among the jewelry, pottery, fabric items, sculpture and various media of framed art they would find there. In addition to the arts and crafts, there would be musicians and food vendors, selling local favorites like conch fritters, lobster rolls, and chocolate-dipped key lime pie on a stick.

For anyone interested in the history of Key West, she described the two maritime museums downtown: the Mel Fisher and the Key West Shipwreck Museum located near the wharf.

The group would next meet together for a fish-fry dinner in the hotel at seven o'clock. That would allow time for anyone you wanted to attend the celebration of the sunset on Mallory Square, first. Jack Burns dryly commented that it would be nice to be eating after dark for a change.

***

AFTER BREAKFAST, the group drifted outside to stand around and chat while waiting for the bus.

Marla Page stood apart from the others, not inviting conversation. Alex hadn't seen much of her since their contentious meeting in the lobby the day before, and wasn't anxious to talk to her now.

Grace and Frances also kept to themselves, keeping their backs to the others as they read their travel brochures. Alex noted with chagrin that Benny the Beaver was dangling from Grace's right hand.

At nine o'clock sharp, a small lavender bus eased up to the curb in front of the C'est La Vie, and swung open its door. Alex made a quick count of those who were standing around, and found that all twelve people were there. That was good, since that was the number she had given to the historical society when she made the arrangements. On the other hand, she was concerned because all of the troublemakers had shown up.

She called out, "We're all here, so let's get on the bus, please. There's plenty of room, so you can

196

spread out and take any seat you want, except for my seat behind the driver. We're only going a few blocks, so don't be concerned with having a view out the windows. Okay? Well, somebody start."

Before anyone else had a chance to react, Marla Page had made a beeline for the bus door and hopped up the stairs. Inside, she headed to the back and sprawled out on the last seat that spanned the width of the bus.

That seemed to challenge Grace, who grabbed Frances and shoved her ahead, cutting off access to the door for the others. After straining a little to get up the high steps, they went halfway back in the bus where Frances dropped into a window seat, and Grace dropped down next to her.

As the others were boarding, Matthew took Alex aside. "Are you sure we'll get back around noon?"

"We should. No later than twelve-fifteen. Why? Do you need to be back at a certain time?"

"Well, Paul Robbins' memorial service is set for one o'clock, and I promised John I'd be there. We've become friends, and I wouldn't want to let him down."

"No, of course not. We should be back in plenty of time. By the way, I'm sorry I missed you and John at the Top of the Key last night. Arlie said he saw you, but by the time we were finished eating, you had left."

Matthew's eyebrows rose in surprise. "I wish I had seen you. It's a very romantic place to have dinner, don't you think?"

Alex caught sight of Flossie giving her a thumbs-up and had to smile at the irony. "It was romantic," she agreed with Matthew. "Well, looks like everyone else has boarded, so after we get on, we'll get on our way."

197

Arlie came up behind her and put his hands on her waist. "Ready?" She nodded and went up the steps as he followed, swinging into the seat behind the driver.

Alex didn't sit, but waited for everyone to get settled. "Okay, we're just going a few blocks up Duval, to Olivia, and then over to the Hemingway house on Whitehead.

"We'll have at least an hour there. After the tour, you'll have time to visit the bookstore and museum, and walk around the one-acre garden. If you'd like, feel free to go up into the lighthouse across the street. Any questions? No? Okay, then, let's go." She nodded to the driver who put the vehicle in gear.

The driver had just started away from the curb when he had to step on the brakes to allow some pedestrians to cross the street in the middle of the block. Cars began to become backed up in both directions. Waiting a minute for the traffic to clear, he started to pull out again, only to have to stomp on the brakes a few seconds later when a two teenage boys stepped out from between parked cars.

Alex gripped the partition in front of her seat. "Geez, some pedestrians take this right-of-way-thing too far, don't they?"

Arlie frowned and shook his head. "Yeah. And if the pedestrian gets hit, it's never his fault … unless it happens on an expressway where it's illegal to walk in the first place."

***

A FEW MINUTES LATER, the bus pulled up in front of the white-painted Spanish Colonial house with the lime-green shutters. Alex called out, "Here we are. We'll go right in for the tour. And don't be shy about

198

asking questions. Tour guides like to be taken off script."

Doyenne Jennie Anders met them in the entryway of the period-furnished home. She started the tour by saying, "Welcome to the home of Ernest Hemingway and his wife Pauline, although they only lived here from 1931 to 1939. Pauline's father bought the home as a wedding gift for the couple, paying only $8,000 in unpaid taxes for it. Later, Pauline would spend $20,000 just to have the pool installed. The house, with its gardens, is still the largest residential property in Key West.

"It was built in 1851 by Asa Tift who made most of his fortune in the shipwreck salvage business. If you go to the Shipwreck Museum, you'll hear all about his adventures, and see some of the treasures from the pirate ships that made Key West the wealthiest city in America in his time.

"We'll start here in the living room. Most of the furniture, accessories, and paintings in the home belonged to the Hemingway's, so you really get a sense of what it was like when he lived and wrote here.

***

AN HOUR AND A QUARTER LATER, the group was again boarding the bus, most of them carrying bags imprinted with the Hemingway Museum logo.

As Joan O'Leary passed by Alex, she gave her a pat on the back. "I learned so much about Hemingway I never knew. Very interesting."

Jack Burns agreed with Joan and added, "With all the personal belongings and a book still open in his study, it was damn spooky. I swear that I sensed his presence."

Alex said, "It must have been even spookier for people who saw you there, as much as you look like him."

After everyone had boarded, Alex got on. "Did you all like that?" There was an enthusiastic response. "Okay, good. We're going on to the Little White House, usually associated with Harry Truman who spent winters there during his presidency. Other presidents used it as a retreat, too. Eisenhower recuperated from his heart attack there, and Kennedy stayed in the house after the invasion of the Bay of Pigs."

"More like a hide-out than a retreat for Kennedy," Ethan O'Leary cracked, as a few people chuckled.

***

TWENTY MINUTES LATER, the lavender bus pulled up in front of the Little White House. It was a two-story white frame home with porches that ran the whole length on both levels. Hurricane shutters covered the walls of windows.

Alex stood up when bus came to a stop. "This is it. Again, we'll go right in for our tour. In the middle of it there will be a short video on the history of the house. After the tour, you'll have plenty of time to visit the museum and stroll around the grounds.

"I see out the window that there are several chickens in the front yard. You may have already seen some walking around in town, as there are a lot of them in Key West. They're considered to be everybody's pets. The first ones were brought here by Cubans in the 19th century when the roosters were used for cock fighting. By the time that was outlawed in the 1970s, many of the owners had moved off the island. The chickens that were left behind were set free, and chickens have been allowed to roam free and reproduce, at will, ever since. Adds to the quirky character of the place.

"Okay, let's get going. We'll meet back at the bus at twelve o'clock sharp."

***

A FEW MINUTES BEFORE TWELVE, Alex and Arlie were sitting in Adirondack chairs in the side yard observing tourists coming and going. As they watched, the Old Town Trolley pulled up to discharge passengers. Alex commented that they should be rounding up their own group and boarding their bus so that they wouldn't be late getting back to the hotel, as she had promised Matthew.

But, just as they got to their feet, they heard screams coming from the street. Breaking into a run they headed down to where some people had gathered around the front end of the trolley.

Arriving at the outside of the crowd, Alex asked the man next to her, "Do you know what happened?"

He answered, "I heard some woman was hit by the trolley as it started up. I don't know if she's badly hurt or what."

Arlie took hold of Alex's arm. "Let's go around these people to the street side so we can make sure it's not one of your people."

Sirens in the distance and honking cars were creating a chaotic, confusing scene. Out on the street, Alex craned her neck to try to make out what was going on at the center of the action where a few people stood in a circle. When one of them moved, she caught her breath as she spied a furry toy. It was Benny the Beaver.

"Grace! Grace!" Alex called out. To the people in front of her she cried out, "One of my people has been hurt! Let us through, please!" As the onlookers stepped back, Alex and Arlie came up to Grace standing there, looking unfazed. Alex clamped a hand on her shoulder. "Grace, what happened? Are you all right?"

Grace nodded in the direction of the trolley. "It's Frances. I think she must of tried to chase away a chicken that had walked into the road. Trolley hit her."

Alex gasped, "Oh, no!"

Arlie tapped a man standing in front of them. "Excuse us, but we need to get to the victim." Alex followed Arlie around the crowd.

Frances was lying on her back with her eyes half closed while a uniformed trolley driver was kneeling next to her.

Alex bent down on her other side. "Frances, it's Alex. How badly are you hurt?"

Frances turned her head towards her. "My shoulder hurts, and my left hip. But I think I'm okay."

Alex looked at the trolley driver whose name tag read, 'Jerry Morton.' "How did it happen that you hit her, Mr. Morton?"

The teary-eyed man shrugged and shook his head. "I don't know! I had just put the trolley in gear. When all of a sudden, this woman was right smack in front of the bus. I slammed on the brakes, but I guess I knocked her down. I've called for an ambulance. There, I hear them now."

They both turned to see flashing lights behind the trolley. In a few moments, a couple of EMTs had rushed up with a gurney.

Alex, Arlie, and the driver stood back to allow the emergency personnel a clear path to Frances. Both EMTs quickly knelt down, asked her a few questions, shone a light in her eyes, and took her pulse and blood pressure. After gently manipulating her limbs, they carefully lifted her onto the gurney.

Once it was raised up, Alex said to one of the EMTs, "This woman's in my tour group. Can you give me a moment?"

"Yeah, okay, but make it quick."

Up close, Alex could see Frances's breathing was shallow and rapid, but was relieved to see that there weren't any visible injuries. "Frances, what were you doing when the trolley hit you?"

Frances tried to look around. "Who all's here?"

Alex answered, "Uh, Arlie, the trolley driver, Grace, and now the EMTs that are taking you to the hospital."

"Oh. Well, I'm not sure how it happened. I just remember standing on the curb, and then the bus hit me and I was dragged on that cow-catcher thing in front. Could you do me a favor? It's important."

"Sure, Frances. What is it?"

"Would you bring Trixie to the hospital? Y'know, just for luck?"

"Uh, okay, if you think that's necessary."

"I do. Promise me." She grabbed Alex's hand.

The young EMT stepped in and eased her aside. "We need to get her to the hospital, ma'am. Her vital signs appear good. I wouldn't worry, but she'll be thoroughly examined in the emergency room. You can check on her later."

Grace walked over to the join them. "I'll ride in the ambulance with her. She's my friend."

"That's a good idea," Alex agreed, nodding to the EMTs. Turning back to Grace, she said, "I'll call your cell after we get back to the hotel. Or you call me when you know something. Here's my card with my number if you don't have it."

The EMTs unlocked the wheels and started towards the ambulance. Frances looked panicky as she was being wheeled away. "Miss Trotter, don't forget about Trixie!"

"All right, Frances. I need to check on something at the hotel, and then I'll bring you the doll. Hopefully, you'll be discharged later this afternoon. I'll have the hotel van pick you up when you are."

Just then, another siren was heard and flashing lights were seen as a squad car pulled up behind the ambulance. The officer who got out spoke briefly with the EMTs as they were placing Frances inside the vehicle. The ambulance was then closed up, the siren turned on, and it took off down Front Street.

The uniformed policeman flipped opened a leather notebook as he strode over to where the trolley driver was standing with Arlie and Alex

Following introductions and a brief exchange, Officer Griggs wanted only Jerry Morton to remain to fill out the incident report.

Walking away, Arlie gave Alex a little squeeze. "It doesn't look like Frances is seriously injured, so let's just wait and see what the doctor says."

Alex looked doubtful. "I know she appeared to be okay, but it's strange that she would insist on me bringing her that stupid doll."

Arlie raised one eyebrow. 'I just said she didn't look injured. I didn't say she wasn't strange."

Saturday afternoon

Chapter 32

ALEX FELT UNNERVED as she stepped down from the bus in front of the hotel. During the entire ride back she had told the group about Frances's accident. In trying to explain how it happened, she had suggested that Frances may have been distracted by a chicken to cause her to step off the curb. As far-fetched as that sounded, she reminded them that their own bus driver had to slam on the brakes twice driving just a few blocks up Duval Street.

As she and Arlie started walking away from the bus, he gently rubbed the back of her neck, "Are you okay? You look a little pale."

"Oh, I'm fine, really. Just shaken up. I mean, who would think I'd have to worry about one of my people getting hit by a bus, for Pete's sake! Like we haven't had enough problems this week?" She turned to face him, tearing up, her mouth twisted in frustration.

He wrapped his arms around her and spoke quietly. "Okay, calm down. Let's deal with one thing at a time." Releasing her he lifted her chin up with his index finger. "You wanna get some lunch? – here − or down the street? It's not yet twelve-thirty, so you have time before you can see your elevator movie."

She started laughing out loud. "That's right, my elevator movie! I mean, isn't this ridiculous? We have to find out if one of my authors is a murderer, and wait to find out if another one has internal injuries after being hit by a bus."

She crossed her eyes and threw up her hands. "Okay, what the hell, let's get lunch. Actually, that might help me put things in a better perspective. Let's just stay in the hotel. We can eat at one of those umbrella tables out back, okay?"

"Sure, whatever you want." They headed up the hotel stairs. "Here, let me get the door for you. You have all those 'burdens' to bear," he teased, giving her a nudge.

Once inside, she paused in the vestibule. "Arlie, let's sit in the lobby for a minute while I call Grace. Just to see how things stand, if she knows anything. That'll clear my mind."

He gestured toward an empty sofa. "Let's sit there. I've always liked a nice chintz."

She sat on one end. "You blew your little 'manly' joke by knowing the word 'chintz,' my friend. Okay, let me call Grace. It'll just take a sec."

Checking a page in her notebook, she punched in a number and waited. "Grace? It's me. Alex. Did you find out anything yet? Uh huh. Uh huh. Okay. Are you staying with her? Good. Tell Frances I'll bring her her doll in an hour or two. Talk to you later. Bye."

"Well?"

"They're admitting her for observation. If nothing else shows up, they'll release her this evening. So far they've seen only bruises and a sprained shoulder. No concussion."

"See? She's not injured. She's just nuts – like I said." He gave a helpless shrug, as though his diagnosis had been only too obvious.

Alex was unzipping a pocket on her purse to replace her phone when she heard a woman's voice that triggered a memory. Looking across the lobby, she recognized the angular figure, sleek head, and signature tortoiseshell glass frames of Lorna Green. The Disney rep was leaning against a mahogany console while she was talking to her assistant, who sat on a low footstool.

Alex felt a chill. She had been sitting on this same sofa once before when she overheard Lorna Green giving instructions to her assistant as they walked through the lobby. What day was that? Tuesday. The day before Fonda Dix was murdered. Something happened then that was a piece of the puzzle to explain what happened to him. It had been a turning point of sorts, but she still couldn't put her finger on it.

Elbowing Arlie, she mumbled out of the side of her mouth, "Pay attention to that woman in the lime green jacket, but don't let her notice you're looking at her."

"Why? Who is she?"

"I'll tell you later. Just listen and follow my lead."

"I don't like the sound of this."

"Shhh! You'll see."

Several people came into the lobby, hauling luggage, to check out at the desk. The commotion temporarily drowned out the conversation between Lorna Green and her assistant. After the travelers left, Alex could hear them again.

"Regina, are you sure you have our tickets?"

"Yes, ma'am, right here in the briefcase."

"Make sure you check again before we leave for the airport. Oh, and don't forget to call George after we know our ETA to have him pick us up at LAX. I don't want to be stuck there in Germ Central any longer than necessary. God knows the plane is bad enough. I'll probably be sitting next to an Ebola nurse. Oh, and don't let me forget to pack a wrap in my carry-on. They could hang meat in those cabins. When do we have to leave for the airport?

"We have three hours before our flight."

"So we'll leave here in about an hour. I don't want to get there too early. The airport's only ten minutes away, and you can print out our boarding passes out when we get there.

"I want to go upstairs to freshen up and take another look around. You can call for a bellhop to take down our bags. God, I'll be glad to get home. Let's go."

Alex gave Arlie a poke. "Okay, it's show time. Just play along. You'll see where I'm going."

Standing, she handed him her notebook and headed across the lobby and left him to follow.

Approaching the two women, she said, "Excuse me, Ms. Green?"

The attractive brunette turned and peered at her through her oversized designer glasses. "Do I know you? If you're a writer, you'll have to have your agent contact my people. I'm just on my way to the airport. Good luck to you." She adjusted her purse strap on her shoulder and started to turn away. "Regina, let's go."

Alex reached out and held her arm. "Ms. Green, I'm not a writer. I'm a tour operator. My name is Alex Trotter, and this is Homicide Detective Arlen Tate."

"What?! *Homicide* Detective. What could a homicide detective possibly want with me?"

Alex calmly regarded her. "We just need a minute of your time to ask you a couple of questions. A man was murdered in the hotel this week —"

"Murdered?!"

Alex started to steer her towards the front of the lobby. "Let's go sit down over there by the window where we can speak privately."

"If you two are setting me up for some kind of hustle to sell me rights to your book or —"

"I'm *not* a writer. Detective Tate, show Ms. Green your I.D."

Arlie took out his badge and flipped it open for Lorna to squint at up close. "Satisfied, Ms. Green?"

She shrugged, giving tacit approval, so Alex continued. "Now, if you and your assistant will just have a seat, this won't take but a couple of minutes. Detective Tate has been asked to investigate the murder of the entertainer, known as Fonda Dix, who worked at the club next door."

"You can't think *I* murdered him! I never even saw the man, much less knew him. In fact, I just heard he had died when I went to his show. They didn't say he had been *murdered*. My God! Should I be getting my lawyer on the phone?" She nodded at Regina.

Alex sighed. "No, please don't. Detective Tate is just checking out some of the people in my tour group who had had disagreements with Mr. Dix. He'll be taking down your statements." She looked pointedly at the notebook, then up at his face.

Taking the hint, Arlie opened the book, took out a pen from his pocket with a flourish, and poised it above a clean page. "Ms. Trotter will ask the questions since she's familiar with the people we're looking at. Go ahead, Ms. Trotter."

Lorna Green seemed to agree with the plan as she turned towards Alex. "Okay. What do you want to know? Let's get it over with."

Alex cleared her throat. "Well, I'm aware that you approached Grace Tuttle with the possibility of using her Benny Beaver books for a Disney project."

Lorna slapped her knee. "Grace Tuttle! I might have known this would involve her. As soon as I met that woman I thought she had only one oar in the water."

"Oh, really? Did you have a problem with her?"

"Well, when I first picked up her books, I thought her little beaver was kinda cute, running around in the forest teaching morality lessons to the other animals. But I warned her that I was worried about using a beaver, since adults often use 'beaver' in a vulgar way. You know what I mean." She shot Arlie a look. "You're not writing all this down, are you?" He shook his head and held up his pen to illustrate he wasn't using it.

Alex smiled benignly. "I'm sure Detective Tate will be discreet. We're only concerned with Grace. So, did she do or say anything to you that you found threatening?"

"Well, she became very defensive and hostile, loudly protesting that she wasn't responsible for all the 'dirty-minded' people in the world, and that the 'evil' use of the word shouldn't be held against her and Benny. She went off into a tirade about 'low-lifes,' or something. She was pretty crazy, when I think about it."

Alex nodded. "How did she leave it with you?"

"Well, let me think. Oh, yes. She said something that didn't make sense, but then, everything she said sounded crazy. She said I shouldn't worry, because I'd never hear a vulgarity like that in any 'nice place' like Key West. This town has like 400 bars. Was she

210

kidding? That could be the mildest thing you'd hear in Key West."

Alex didn't react. "You had another meeting with Grace when you told her you couldn't use Benny for another reason, right?"

"She must have told you. Yeah, our legal department shit bricks when I faxed them a picture of Benny. I had been only concerned that the puppet was commercially sold. I didn't know that he was *Disney's trademark icon* for some toothpaste that hasn't been sold since 1973. That's before I was born, for God's sake!

"Anyway, when I explained why we couldn't use her beaver, she completely flipped out. She said I didn't know what she had 'gone through' to get this deal. *I* was the one who had embarrassed myself in front of the whole legal department of Disney, and she thought *she* had something to complain about?

"But what does any of this have to do with the murder of that Fonda Dix? If you need me to confirm that Grace was with me for part of Tuesday and Wednesday afternoons, I'll do that. Renee must have the exact times, if there's some question. The woman's a whacko, but I don't think she's a murderer.

"Anyway, if that's all, we have to get upstairs to finish packing and get to the airport."

Alex stood up with Lorna. "That's all we need, Ms. Green. Thank you. And safe travels."

After the two women departed, Arlie said, "Okay, I know what you were getting at, but it's all circumstantial, and doesn't prove anything. A District Attorney would never take this to court at this point."

"I'll explain the significance of what Lorna Green said later. Right now we have to watch that video. I now know what to look for."

Saturday afternoon

Chapter 33

ALEX GLANCED OVER AT the front desk. No sign of Mr. Hudson. Chrissie seemed to be the only clerk on duty, but she was waiting on a hotel guest, while another man stood in line.

Alex checked her watch and saw that it was a little after one. Manager Hudson should have gone home by now. Looking at Chrissie waving her arms around, she was probably giving directions to some restaurant or tourist attraction, which shouldn't take long.

Arlie took hold of her elbow. "Let's go to lunch, okay?"

Alex looked over at the desk again. "Wait a minute. Chrissie should be free in a couple of minutes, and Mr. Hudson is gone, so the coast is clear. But we shouldn't just stand here. Let's sit down and read a magazine so we don't attract attention."

Arlie leaned over and picked up a couple magazines off the coffee table. "There's only *Southern*

Living and *Women's Health.* I might look more suspicious if I'm reading these."

Alex made a little growling sound. "Just open one to a page that doesn't picture pregnant women doing exercises, or has photographs comparing chandeliers, and you'll be fine."

They sat down in chairs where Alex could still see the desk. Picking up a health magazine, she found an article on macro diets, while Arlie gamely flipped through pages until he found one on real estate values in southern urban areas, which he started to read.

After a few minutes, Alex glanced over to the front desk. Chrissie was still behind the counter, but there weren't any guests waiting for her. When Alex caught her eye, Chrissie waved her over.

Alex jumped to her feet. "Chrissie's ready for us. Let's go!"

Arlie closed the magazine and looked up at her. "I'm guessing this puts lunch on a permanent hold."

As he stood, she tugged at his arm. "Don't forget, our story is that one of my people had a gold watch stolen out of his pocket when he was on the elevator."

"Well, you know we're not going to see *that.*"

"Don't worry. I've got this one. Just follow my lead, again."

"Right. I'll just follow you around, staying two steps behind." Alex made a face, and punched him lightly on the arm.

As they approached the front desk, Chrissie looked warily at Arlie and then back at Alex, who quickly spoke up. "This is Detective Arlie Tate, Chrissie. He's helping me investigate the theft of the watch."

The clerk's eyes became large and round. Leaning over the counter she spoke in a low, but urgent, voice. "I thought this was just between us. I told you Mr. Hudson wouldn't like me showing the tape to you, and now you've gone and gotten the police involved!"

Alex shook her head and waved off Chrissie's anxiety. "Don't worry. Arlie is my boyfriend. I asked him to look at the video with me so he could advise me if I see who took my client's watch."

Chrissie looked dubiously at Arlie, who cracked a friendly smile. "Alex is right. I'm not here as a cop. If you let us take a look at the half hour or so of the tape she's interested in, we won't need to take any more of your time.

"Look, I understand your reluctance to let us see the hotel's private tapes, but I assure you that you're doing the right thing to help out the victim of a crime."

Chrissie smiled weakly. "All right. Let's just do this. It's all set it up in our office. Now would be a good time, since no one's around.

She studied his face for a moment. "I must say that you're both very intent to find some guy who stole a watch.

"Anyway, go to the door down the wall and I'll let you in."

Following her directive, they were let into the office and sat in the two folding chairs that had been set up to watch a small TV on the desk.

Chrissie picked up and cradled two video tapes on her outstretched palms like they were sacred texts. "Well, here are the ones that cover Wednesday morning, between seven and nine. The images are a little fuzzy on our system, but hopefully you can see well enough."

Alex carefully took the tapes from her.

"And here's the remote, Detective. I have to go back to the desk, so just come out when you're ready, okay?"

"Perfect," Alex said. "We shouldn't be long. Thanks again for your help."

As the door closed, Alex clutched the tapes to her chest, beaming. "This is it! This is the last piece of the puzzle. That is, unless I'm totally off base, in which case I don't have a clue as to how Fonda Dix was murdered."

Arlie pried one of the tapes out of her hand, slipped it into the slot on the player, and held up the remote. "All right, 'Show time!' as you would say."

As the image of the interior of the elevator appeared on the screen, they both were relieved to see that the camera lens captured all four walls.

The date, hour, minutes, and seconds ran across the top of the picture. The first frame read: Wednesday, January 21, 7:00 a.m. and 0 seconds. It then counted off each second after that in real time.

As the tape played, Alex sat hunched over the desk, her hands balled into fists, as she scrutinized the images of strangers that got on and off the elevator. It was amazing how long a second was when you looked at a clock that ticked seconds off one by one. And she was surprised that it took only about two minutes for the elevator to make a regular run from the top to the bottom. She would have guessed that it took at least five minutes, based on how long it felt when you were on it.

When the tape read 7:25 and 27 seconds, Alex had to blink to clear her vision after having stared at the screen so intently for half an hour. But, then, her eyes focused like lasers as Flossie and Cynthia boarded when the elevator stopped on the second floor. She felt shivers going up her spine as she realized that this was the beginning of the time-line scenario that she had imagined.

The car remained on the second floor for a few seconds as Ethan and Joan stepped in and greeted the two women. Then, someone's hand was in the picture holding the door open. As the man came into view, she saw that he was someone she didn't know. She could lip-read that he said, "You're welcome" as Virgil Meade came into the picture, hurrying to get in.

On the rest of the way down, Virgil was the only one talking. She couldn't make out what he said, but thought she might not have been able to make sense of it even if there *had* been sound.

"Do you recognize those people, Arlie?"

"Yeah, sure. Virgil, Flossie, that romance writer, the O'Learys. Why? Are they significant?"

"Yes, because the timing of their appearance fits with what I thought happened before I came downstairs on Wednesday. All five of them were already in the dining room when I walked in."

"Okay. So this confirms your memory. Anything else?"

"No, but watch carefully and get ready to stop the tape. Ready?"

"I'm ready. I'm ready."

The time on the tape was 7:32 and 17 seconds when the empty elevator arrived on the third floor. Two women she didn't recognize got on and pushed the 'down' button. Alex figured they knew one another as they were chatting on the way to the second floor.

"Watch now, Arlie. Get ready to hit 'pause.'"

The doors opened on the second floor. Alex started tearing up as she saw Paul Robbins and John Austin step into the cab.

"That's Paul in the blue shirt with John!"

"I see them. I'm watching everything."

A man's hand could then be seen holding the door open for someone else as he remained outside. He continued to hold it open for three second before anyone else came into the picture. Two women then came into view.

Alex gasped as she watched the woman with a scarf tied around her head push Frances Primm into the car, and then turn to speak to the man holding the door. He then released it and stepped back to let the car go down without him.

"Oh, my God, Arlie. Look!"

The woman in the headscarf elbowed her way past the two women from the 3rd floor to get to the back of the elevator where she remained, pressed against Paul Robbins.

Within three seconds, Alex could see Benny Beaver's nose materialize between the woman and Paul, and watched in horror as the furry creature was being held against Paul's midsection.

"Pause it there, Arlie!"

"Son-of-a-bitch," Arlie murmured. "What the hell are we looking at here? Does she have that puppet holding a hypodermic needle?"

"No, Arlie. She has a hypodermic needle in her hand *inside the puppet* and she is shooting some anesthetic from one needle, and some air out of another through Benny's mouth and into one of Paul's arteries."

Arlie gaped at the screen, leaning forward. "Holy shit! We're actually watching her murder the guy right in front of five other people who aren't even aware of what's going on. This is unbelievable."

"Put it on 'play' again, Arlie. We have to make sure we can identify Grace, not that there's any doubt."

The tape continued running. At 7:32 and 21 seconds they saw Paul Robbins grimace and put his hand over his heart. Everyone else in the elevator kept looking straight ahead, including Grace, whose face was now visible. Visible and unmistakable.

217

"We've got her, Arlie! We've got her! Keep the tape running."

The elevator continued its descent. At 7:33 and 46 seconds it stopped on the main floor, and the doors opened. The two women from the 3rd floor got off first and resumed their conversation. Frances took one step out of the car, and paused. Grace could be seen in the back undoing her headscarf and wrapping it around her right hand. Then she bolted out of the car, and pulled Frances along with her. John turned to Paul in response to something he had said. John's face became creased with concern, and Paul had turned grey, as the two men exited the car and out of view of the camera.

The elevator sat empty with its doors open.

Alex turned to Arlie. "I hate to say I told you so, but…"

"You can say it as often as you want to. This is one for the books. When did you know, and how were you so sure?"

"Well, as I've told you, Grace was the only person with any motive that I knew of. Then, when you and I sat down on the chintz sofa, and I saw Lorna Green, I had a flashback to Tuesday afternoon when I witnessed a similar scene.

"I thought that something had happened then that was connected to the murder. Reliving that moment, it came back to me. Lorna had told her assistant that they would be going to the 'Some Like It Hot" show the next night, and I repeated that to Grace. She seemed to be distraught after I told her what I overheard Lorna say, but, since she was usually in a bad mood, I didn't attach any significance to it. I thought she was just upset that Lorna Green was staying at the same hotel.

"Then, when we talked to Lorna Green today, she said that she told Grace she was leery about using a beaver in a children's movie because of the vulgar jokes about beavers. Grace's response was that she wouldn't hear anything like that in 'nice places like Key West.'

"I was there Tuesday morning when Paul whispered something to Grace at breakfast that shocked her. I later learned that he was getting a beaver puppet, and that's obviously what he had told Grace.

"When I told Grace that Lorna would be at the club when Paul would be doing jokes Grace knew would be with his new beaver puppet, she planned to kill him the next morning.

Lorna Green was the one who supplied the real motive for Grace killing Paul. I knew that Grace wouldn't stop at murder in order to save her deal with Disney, but I hadn't known before how Paul could have done something to squelch the deal.

"When it fell through on Thursday because of the trademark infringement, Grace was beside herself. That's why she got drunk on the dinner cruise and ranted at John about how evil he and Paul were. It was her way of justifying her killing Paul when he had nothing to do with her losing the Disney deal. If he didn't deserve to be murdered for ruining her future, she reasoned that he deserved to be murdered because he was an immoral influence in the world.

"I guess that's all of it." She leaned back and exhaled a long stream of air.

Arlie pulled her towards him and kissed her cheek. "That is one twisted story that you unraveled, babe. And now Grace is a free woman, sitting in the hospital where an autopsy proved Paul had been murdered by the injection of air that caused an arterial embolism.

"We need to notify the police to have her picked up. We'd better get to the hospital ourselves, and make sure she's still there."

Alex leaned in towards him. "Oh, first I have to get that silly doll to take to Frances. She was insistent that I not forget." She tilted her head, coyly. "Um, I know I should get a cleaning woman to go into her room but, you know, that hypodermic needle is probably still there…"

Arlie put a finger to her lips. "Which is the very reason we won't go near that room without a warrant. We don't want that evidence to be thrown out because of an illegal search and seizure."

"Okay, okay. Don't worry. I don't want to do anything to screw things up at this point. I'll get the hotel staff to go in and get the doll."

"Good. It shouldn't take you long. In the meantime, I'll call the station and talk to the detective assigned to the investigation. Ha! This will be the sweetest case that sonovabitch has ever worked."

Saturday afternoon

Chapter 34

UP ON THE SECOND FLOOR, Alex located the room where Grace and Frances were staying. Following the whine of a vacuum cleaner, she went further along the corridor and peeked into the room being cleaned. Attracting the attention of the young dark-haired woman who was changing the sheets, she motioned for her to come out into the hallway.

"Sí, señora?"

"You speak English?"

"Sí, señora.

"Uh, right. Well, let me try to show you what I want." Pointing to the room's door handle, she made a show of turning it, and the pointed at the woman, and then back to the handle, saying, "I need you to go into my amigo's room, numero two-one-five, and get her doll." She clasped her arms and swung them back and forth like she was rocking a baby.

The housekeeper's eyes got as big as saucers. "Su amigo dejado a su bebé en su cuarto habitación?!"

Running back into the room where her co-worker was still vacuuming, she cried out, "Dios mío. ¡ Ven rápido! Amigo de esta mujer dejado a su bebé solo en su habitación. Tenemos que rescatarlo! ¡ Ven rápido!"

Alex ran after her waving her arms. "No! I think you misunderstood. There's no emergencia! No emergencia! It's just a doll!" She repeated the rocking movement."

The other woman dropped the nozzle she was using. "¿Ha quedado un bebé? Llamamos a la policía?"

Alex grabbed her by the shoulders. "Wait a minute! You said police. No police! We don't need the police. It's just a doll. Not a baby. A *doll-o*." She got down on her knees, and repeated the cradling movement. "See? A niño's baby – a doll-o."

The two cleaning women looked at each other, their foreheads creased in confusion. "Doll-o?" one asked the other who raised her hands in bewilderment.

Then the first woman's face brightened in recognition. "Oh, lo sé. Refiere a una muñeca. Una muñeca."

Turning to Alex, she asked, "Una muñeca como Barbie?"

Alex smacked her forehead. "Yes! Like Barbie! A moonyeca like Barbie."

She motioned for them to follow her down the hallway. Again, they checked with each other to interpret. After a moment, they shrugged, in a "Why not?" manner and took off behind her.

Getting to the door with the numerals 215 on it, Alex again pantomimed turning the handle to enter, but this time added the word, "moonyeca."

The two cleaners nodded that they understood. The older cleaning woman unlocked the door, and the younger woman disappeared inside. A few seconds later she re-emerged with Trixie in tow.

Alex thought the doll looked irritated at being abducted from her comfortable resting place, but she slowly reached out and gingerly took her, turning her around to face forwards. Bowing to the two women, Alex effused, "Gracias. Muchas gracias," and took off for the elevator before they had a chance to question anything.

In the elevator she sighed heavily and thought, ruefully, that this was supposed to be the easy part of the plan to get to the hospital to hold onto Grace.

Walking into the lobby, she saw that Arlie was still sitting where she had left him.

He looked up as she approached. "I see you got the doll. Any problems?"

"It's a long story. Let's just say you shouldn't play Charades with people who don't speak English, particularly when you need to distinguish between a 'doll' and a 'baby.' Alex set Trixie down next to him. "Did you get through to the right detective?"

"Yeah. Joe Karns. I think at first he thought I was a crank caller. Seems he just got the case. Said he had read that it was a death by natural causes, and then, saw that the autopsy found it to be murder. Today, I call and inform him that I have a videotape of the crime. He's sending a couple uniforms to the hospital to arrest Grace. Are you ready to go?"

"Yeah. I'm just wondering what part Frances played in all this. She was there getting into the elevator with Grace when she killed Paul. But, Frances was taking her time getting out of the elevator when they got down to the main floor. And then, I wonder about her mental state that she insists on having Trixie brought to her at the hospital when she's only there for observation."

Arlie peered down at the doll. "What's that in her dress pocket?"

223

"What?"

"That paper sticking up."

She pulled it out and unfolded it. Holding it up, she read, "'If anything happens to me, Grace did it.'

"Oh, my God! Arlie, why didn't I see that Frances was in danger?! Grace thinks she's gotten away with murder. Frances either knew from the beginning, or figured it out, so Grace can't let her live.

"Frances wasn't trying to save some chicken when she got hit. It was Grace who pushed her into the path of the trolley to try to kill her! And I let Grace go with her to the hospital where she'd have her choice of methods. Frances couldn't tell me she was afraid because Grace was standing right there, so she had me get Trixie to find her message. We have to go to save her, if we're not already too late!"

Saturday afternoon

Chapter 35

ALEX SNATCHED UP TRIXIE before she and Arlie raced out of the hotel and jumped in a cab, startling the driver by ordering him to drive to the hospital on the double.

Ten minutes later, they were walking up to the front desk at the Lower Keys Medical Center where they asked for the room number of a Frances Primm.

The silver-haired female volunteer glanced up from her computer and quickly sized up the situation. "Oh. Our children's unit is on the third floor. You can take that elevator over there. They'll help you when you get there."

"Frances Primm is not a child," Alex replied testily. "Listen, we need to find her immediately. Her life is in danger!"

"Oh, I'm sure she's being well cared for, miss. We have excellent doctors here." She scanned sheets of paper. "Let me see … Primm, is it? I don't see that we have anyone admitted by that name."

Arlie leaned over the counter to lock eyes with the receptionist. "Frances isn't technically an admission. She's here for observation, if that helps."

"Oh, yes, that does help! I have a separate list for 'Observations." She pulled out another sheet of paper. "Okay, now, Primm, Primm. Here it is. Frances Primm, room 142. That's right down that hall." She pointed to her left.

They started off in that direction as she called after them, "Good luck, but I'm sure she'll be fine!"

Hurrying down the hallway, they passed other patients' rooms, all with open doors, until they came to one closed door with the number 142 on it. Arlie reached for the handle, but Alex caught his arm to caution him. "Maybe Frances is changing."

He pulled down on the handle. "And maybe she isn't." He pushed open the door and strode inside with Alex behind him, holding Trixie out in front of her as a message to Frances.

At the far end of the two-bed room they pulled up short when they saw Frances wrapped in white sheeting, hooked up to an IV drip, as Grace held onto her wrist where the plastic tubing was inserted.

Seeing them, Frances cried out, "Detective! Miss Trotter! Grace is going to put something in my IV to kill me!"

Grace smiled benignly, displaying her menacing front teeth. "Nonsense. I'm just helping her get some rest. Nothing to get upset about. Anyway, this doesn't concern either of you. Please just put down the doll and leave. I'm a professional nurse, so I know what I'm doing."

Arlie moved a little closer to the bed. "Oh, we're well aware that you know what you're doing, Grace. In fact, we have it on videotape."

"What are you talking about?"

"I'm talking about when you made sure you were in a crowded elevator with Fonda Dix to inject him through Benny's mouth with anesthetic and a syringe full of air."

Frances raised herself up on her elbows, but was roughly shoved back down. Turning her head, she whimpered, "I figured out that she killed Fonda Dix, and now she's going to kill me. Please, stop her!"

Arlie edged closer to the bed. "What's in the vial, Grace?"

Grace held up a small clear bottle in the light coming through the window, gazing lovingly at it. "It's just propofol. It'll put her to sleep."

Alex gasped. "Arlie, that's what killed Michael Jackson!"

He turned slightly and held up his hand. Taking the hint, she bit down on her lower lip to stay quiet, and sank down on the unoccupied bed.

Extending a hand towards Grace, he urged, "C'mon, give me the vial, Grace. It's all over. We know you murdered Fonda Dix."

Grace stared him down with narrowed eyes. "That's crazy! He died of a heart attack. Everybody knows that."

Arlie held her gaze. "You left a puncture mark on the abdomen, Grace, and the autopsy showed that he had suffered a massive heart attack caused by an arterial gas embolism. The one *you* injected. I've reported all this to the police. They're on their way here to arrest you. And, I bet, when we look at Benny over there, we'll find a couple of punctures in his mouth."

Grace sneered. "You're talking crazy. I don't believe anything you're saying. You came here just to bring Trixie, like Frances asked you. And now you both need to go. If you don't leave in five seconds, I will give her a fatal dose of the propofol."

Arlie didn't look away. "You will anyway. Don't make it worse for yourself, Grace."

Just then, the sound of knocking drew everyone's attention to the doorway as a pudgy blond nurse breezed in. "Who called from the empty bed?" she demanded.

During the momentary distraction, Arlie closed the gap between himself and Grace, and grabbed her from behind, pinning her arms to her sides while she thrashed around trying to bite him.

The nurse stood there frozen with her mouth open. "What's going on here?" she asked in a small voice.

Alex jumped up. "That woman is trying to kill Frances with propofol."

Hearing footsteps from out in the hallway, they all looked up as two uniformed officers filled the doorway, barging into the room. They both had their hands on their holstered service weapons. "Police! Stay where you are!"

Seeing Arlie restraining the writhing Grace, the two cops approached. "Grace Tuttle?" one asked.

Arlie answered, "This is Grace."

The older one announced in a commanding voice, "Grace Tuttle, I'm placing you under arrest for murder. You have the right to remain silent, but anything you say or do may be used against you in a court of law. You have the right to an attorney before being questioned. If you cannot afford one, one will be assigned to you. Do you understand your rights as I have explained them?"

Grace spat out, "I understand that you're out of your fucking mind!"

The nurse still hadn't moved. In a breathy voice she exclaimed, "I've never seen such a fast response to a crime!"

Alex scoffed. "It's not *this* crime she's being arrested for. It's for an earlier murder this week. She's been busy."

Arlie reached in his pocket, took out his I.D, and showed it to the officers before handing Grace over to them. After they had secured her with handcuffs, Arlie said, "We're also alleging that she attempted to murder this woman, Frances Primm. Before we walked in, Grace was ready to dispense a fatal dose of propofol in her port. And, earlier today, she pushed her in the path of a moving trolley."

One of the cops looked at Arlie, scratching his head. "What's this all about, anyway?"

Arlie replied with a smirk, "She wanted her beaver puppet to be in a Disney movie to teach morality lessons to children."

Sunday morning

Chapter 36

AFTER BREAKFAST THE NEXT MORNING, the members of the group started carrying their luggage down to store in a room behind the front desk. After checking out, they would still have a few hours before they needed to leave for the airport.

Gathering in the lobby, Flossie, Cynthia, Adeline, Ethan, Joan, Virgil, Matthew, Frances, Alex, Jack and Neil LeRoy, were still talking about the murderous acts of Grace Tuttle, and the last-second rescue of Frances Primm.

Frances had become the object of everyone's sympathies. She had joined them for dinner, after being discharged from the hospital, and answered their many questions as they dined on fried fish.

In relating her story, she told them about how she had been drawn into Grace's paranoia, believing that Fonda Dix's crude humor had threatened her Disney deal.

And after he told her at breakfast on Tuesday that he was getting a beaver puppet that day for his act; and Alex told her that Lorna Green would be at the club to see it, Grace had said that she would find a way to stop him.

Had Frances known that Grace was planning on killing him in the elevator? No. Grace had told her that she was going to inject him with something that would make him only a little nauseous for a couple of days. Just sick enough so that he couldn't do the show while Lorna Green was in town.

She explained that she and Grace had gotten up early on Wednesday and waited in the second hallway where they could look around the corner for Fonda to come out of his room. Then they followed him to the elevator to ride down with him.

Didn't she realize that Grace had killed him when she heard that he died? No, because Grace explained it away, saying that the nausea must have brought on a heart attack due to his having a bad heart. She said that it could have happened at any time. It was a coincidence.

When did she figure out the truth? When she saw that Grace wasn't surprised that Fonda Dix had died, and was even happy about it, she had to consider that Grace intentionally murdered him.

She had confronted Grace with her suspicions when Grace got drunk on the night of the dinner cruise, and Grace had admitted it. Then Grace threatened to kill her if she ever told anyone, and that she'd do it in a way that would appear to be an accident or by natural causes. Frances had seen her get away with one murder already, so she knew that her days were numbered. As a safeguard, she put the note in Trixie's pocket yesterday morning before the sightseeing tour.

After Frances's story, Arlie shared what part Alex had played: ordering an autopsy to prove that Fonda Dix had been murdered, and viewing the elevator tape from the morning Paul died to prove how and by whom.

As they sat around the lobby going over it all again, Arlie came in with a burly man with a crewcut, wearing an ill-fitting linen sports coat. "Frances, this is Detective Joe Karns. He's working the Dix homicide and needs to ask you some questions at the station."

Frances appeared unnerved as she stood and extended a shaky hand.

"Don't worry, ma'am. This won't be difficult. But first, I need your permission to enter the room you shared with the accused. Since you have control of the property, it'll save me getting a warrant for access to let CSI collect evidence.

"Okay," Frances agreed, uncertainly. "Grace wouldn't like that, though, I know."

"Grace is in jail and she's not going anywhere anytime soon. You won't have to see her or communicate with her. Detective Tate will come up with us so that you feel more comfortable."

After the three of them left, Marla Page appeared in the doorway and staggered in with two canvas bags, each one having a copy of her book, *Screaming Bloody Murder,* visible on top. "Idiot porters disappear when you have to haul anything to check out," she groused. "Watch these bags, will you? I'll be right back." She set down them down in the middle of the floor and flounced over to the front desk, as the others shared looks of disapproval.

Marla finished checking out and returned to her bags, just as the front door opened admitting a dark-haired woman with a white streak in her hair.

Alex jumped up. "Vera Blaze!"

Vera looked around at the sound of her name. "Oh, Miss Trotter! I'm glad you're still here. I need to see Marla Page."

Alex automatically glanced at Marla who was just picking up her bags. Vera followed her eyes, taking in what Alex was looking at.

"You!" Vera cried out. "You're the one who stole my book, *Screams in the Night,* and renamed it, *Screaming Bloody Murder!"*

Marla twisted her mouth into an ugly snarl. "Who are you? I don't know you!"

Vera's eyes flashed. "Well, you soon will! I've consulted an attorney who tells me that the court has ordered damages for piracy for up to $150,000, and that was for far less than you've pirated. I'm here to give you notice that I have started the process of suing you, I won't stop until you have paid for stealing my story. It was my *own personal story*! I was the one who was raped! How dare you steal my vengeance from me!"

Marla tried to ignore her by picking up one of her bags. Vera rushed at he and tried pulling it away from her. Marla took a deep breath, found a footing against the other bag, and yanked on the one in her hand, just as Vera let go, causing Marla to fall backwards, sprawled out on the floor. In the melee, the bags had been upended, spilling out their contents.

At this point everyone in the lobby had encircled the two women, and were in shock as they looked at the dozens of softcover books that lay spread out on the dark hardwood floor.

Vera picked up a few of them and glared down at Marla. "I bet you stole all of these!" Checking the covers she said, "I know some of these people. They're new authors who have just published their own books. You steal the books, and then you steal their ideas, don't you!"

Marla scrambled to her feet, ran at Vera, and started pounding on her with her fists. "Get out of here, you bitch!"

Joan O'Leary, who was standing behind Marla, grasped her and pulled her back. "Marla, stop it! This woman sounds like she has a valid complaint. And, why don't you tell us how you got all of these books? At $15 a copy, you must have $300 - $400 in books here."

The front door opened, attracting everyone's attention, as two police officers rushed in. "Police!" one of them called out.

The older officer, taking stock of the scene, eyed the two disheveled women and the piles of books on the floor, said, "Okay, ladies, let's break it up. The hotel called about there being a disturbance here in the lobby."

Vera Blaze brushed some of her white hair out of her eyes. "This woman stole my book. Not a copy of it, but all of the text. I've seen a lawyer, and I'm suing for piracy. I just came over to tell her that and I found out she's stolen copies of other people's books."

The younger officer turned to Marla. "Is that true?"

Marla straightened her blouse. "No, of course not. I'm the one who's been physically attacked, as you can plainly see."

"I'd like to see the receipts for all these books, ma'am, the older policeman countered.

"I have better things to do than keep track of receipts for everything," Marla answered, indignantly.

In response, he took hold of her arm and started pulling her towards the door. "Well, why don't we all go down to the station and sort this out. If that's convenient, of course."

Arlie came back into the lobby as the police were ushering Marla and Vera out to the waiting squad car. Crossing over to join Alex, he said under his breath, "If the police haul off any more of your people, you'll just need a cab to take everyone to the airport."

Overhearing, Neil LeRoy chuckled. "I just want to be the one who writes this book. I don't think I even need to embellish the story. It's got jealousy, rage, revenge, greed, and, last of all, murder. I guess I just need to add some sex and I'll have a best seller."

Arlie smiled and nodded. Taking Alex's hand, he said, "Let's get away from this crime wave and go walk on the beach."

Saturday, late morning

Chapter 37

THE SHORE WAS CROWDED by the time that Alex and Arlie got there. "Let's go down further where there aren't so many people," he suggested.

She took off her sandals and dug her feet into the cool, soft sand. "Ooh, this is so nice. Good idea to come here for a walk, Arlie."

When they had strolled far enough that there weren't any more people, he wrapped his arms around her from behind and gazed out at the turquoise water. "I thought we'd have more time like this, but I should have known better with any group of yours."

She playfully socked him on his forearm. "Not *any* group. But I can't argue with you about this group. I'm just so grateful that you flew down to join me."

Arlie rested his chin on the top of her head. "You know, I don't think we should continue flying back and forth to see each other all the time."

Alex tried to twist her head. "What?! You don't want to fly to see me?"

"No. I think we should be living in the same place."

Alex exhaled a long breath of air. "You know, you really should watch how you put things. I thought you were breaking up with me. And what, may I ask, are you saying exactly, that we should be living in the same place – the same state? The same city? The same house?"

"Well, I'm thinking, the same house."

She turned to face him. "Arlie, is this a proposal?"

"Yes, but apparently not a very good one if you can't tell. I knew I'd screw this up. Anyway, I love you, and I want to marry you. If you agree, of course."

"Arlie Tate. As I've said many times, you never fail to surprise me. Of *course* I want to marry you, you big goof."

He grinned sheepishly before holding her face up to give her a long, tender kiss.

As they broke apart, he fumbled in his pocket. "Well, good so far, but I have something here for you. Okay, I've got it." He opened a small square box and extracted a sparkly ring. Holding it out, he eased it onto her third finger.

Alex had tears in her eyes as she gazed at the brilliant round diamond surrounded by smaller cut sapphires. "It's really beautiful, Arlie. And it fits. How did you know my ring size?"

"I'm a detective, remember? I slipped on a sizing tape when you were sleeping. I thought the sapphires matched your eyes. Sorta. Well, better than rubies."

She held her hand up, again. "It's perfect! This is all so amazing, and unexpected, I don't even know

237

what to start thinking about it. Like, where do you think we should live?"

Arlie dug his hands in his pocket. "Well, I didn't think you'd want to live in coastal Georgia. I mean, you've always lived in Chicago."

Alex brightened. "Do you mean that you'd move to Chicago? You know, with the high murder rate we have you'd be assured of being hired by the Chicago PD as a homicide detective. You'd have more work than you could handle."

Arlie looked up at the clouds. "I doubt that the Chamber of Commerce uses their high crime rate as an attraction for job-seekers."

He paused a moment. "I was wondering what you would think about maybe moving to Atlanta. It's urban, like you're used to, and since my parents live there, my mother could help to get your business going with referrals to friends in their club."

Alex pursed her lips in thought. "I can maybe see moving to Atlanta. It does seem like a reasonable compromise."

"With your dad taking photographs for the magazines he works for in Paris, it could be a while before they return to the United States. I thought it would be nice for us to be near some family."

"You have thought this through. And, yes, I'd like that, too. So, when did you think we should get married?"

Arlie put his hands on her shoulders. "If you'd have enough time to plan things, I thought maybe this spring. If we're married in Atlanta, you couldn't find a better party planner than my mother."

Alex grinned. "That works for me. I wouldn't want to ask my mom to come from Paris just to help me book a hall and pick out flowers.

"Oh, I'll have to tell Beth, my roommate."

"Yes. She might notice when you're not in the apartment anymore." He clucked her under the chin. "My one concern is going on a honeymoon with you, considering what happens on your trips."

"The only times there have been problems are when you're along."

"My point, exactly. Seriously, I thought we'd visit Paris, first, so we could spend a few days with your parents. I'll have a chance to get to know them, and you'll have time to visit before we leave for the south of France. What do you think?"

"I think it'll be the best trip I ever planned. You know, it'll be just the two of us on our honeymoon. What could possibly go wrong?"

.

ACKNOWLEDGMENTS

Many thanks to my good friends at G J Publishing, John Neilans, and author Marilyn Smith Neilans, for their many contributions to this book.

Marilyn first suggested that Key West would make an ideal setting for one of my mysteries in my "Vacation Murders" series. From her own experience, she described the historic La Te Da Hotel on Duval Street, and its adjoining club that features female impersonators, which became the basis for my C'est La Vie Hotel and the Some Like It Hot lounge.

After they received my finished manuscript, both John and Marilyn applied their editorial and publishing skills to improve the formatting, as well as to proofread and edit the text to make grammatical corrections and smooth out the prose.

Also, many thanks to my husband Jim who acted as an invaluable "first reader" of the rough draft of each chapter. His comments on my plot and characters improved both aspects in great measure. I counted on him to spot any writing that became too "precious," a literary device that didn't work, or any inconsistencies.